THE LITURGY
OF
FATHER EDWARD

Kate Hiller

A novel written with
Chris Baker

THE LITURGY OF FATHER EDWARD

Kate Hiller

A novel written with
Chris Baker

For Chris's mother, father, and seven siblings.

The vocation of humanity is to show forth the image of God
and to be transformed into the image of the Father's only
Son.

1877, Catechism of the Catholic church

Chapter 1

The clock read 5:38 a.m., and he knew it was now or never to fit in his morning cigarette. He sloppily dressed in the dark and avoided the floorboards closest to Alice's room as he hurried past. No matter how early he was up, his housekeeper was up even earlier. The old house couldn't be trusted with secrets, and he had to use the front door, the only one that didn't sag in protest.

Edward felt his blood pressure rise as he rounded the house to the back. Surely the neighbors wouldn't be up this early as well? What is it about that family that they can never be quiet? If it wasn't their little girl pestering him with questions, it was their dog barking at the neighbor's cat. Of all people, he shouldn't be judging the poor, but their constant clamor kept the words ringing true—"the poor will always be with us."

"Oh blast," Edward thought, "I forgot my glasses and I can't see a thing. I hope she doesn't sneak up on me."

Edward's head was pounding by the time he lit his cigarette. He hid behind the overgrown lilac near the rubbish bins. His headache made him regret the second glass of wine last night. Mrs. Pedigraw always insisted he have one more after dinner. Her husband was usually bored with the conversation by the time she was stacking the dishes, and Mrs. Pedigraw seemed to come alive just as soon as he retired to his easy chair.

"Thomas doesn't share our fondness for wine," Mrs. Pedigraw had crooned as she looked at the wine label. "This is the latest and I think it is their best yet, don't you?"

Edward had nodded, hoping the wine would curb his annoyance with her. He suspected that it was more than duty fueling Mrs. Pedigraw's weekly invite, and he was growing weary of it. He had heard it all before—how nobody else was signing up for the parish suppers and who in the directory was secretly using birth control.

"Thomas and I just weren't able to have children, that's all. We accepted it as a sign from the Lord that, instead of raising children, we were to feed our shepherd regularly and always bring extra food to the potlucks. I am so tired of seeing the large families barely bring enough to feed themselves. That goes against the potluck rules, you know—always bring at least a couple more servings beyond what is needed to feed your own family. And, how hard is it to bring both a dessert and a side dish?"

The tension had increased in Edward's head as he imagined it all—families entering the church hall with babies in arms, toddlers at their heels, pre-teens carrying crockpots, tripping over loose cords, and older women fussing over their Jello molds. Did the children really outnumber the casserole dishes?

About the time that Thomas called for his wife to bring him his second beer, Edward was planning his exit. If he made it home by 7:30, Alice might be making her evening phone call to her son, and it was a perfect time to have one more cigarette before sneaking past her to his room. Then he could retire for the night and read more of Brother Lawrence, whose words recently were the only thing keeping him sane.

He tried to focus on some of the words he had read last, "I am not praying for relief—I am praying for strength."

"Thank you for the fine evening and dinner, Mrs. Pedigraw. Deacon McElway has some papers he needed me to read through. Please pass along my gratitude to your husband." Edward put the table between himself and his hostess and quickly headed for the door. Mrs. Pedigraw somehow got around the table in time to grab his hand.

"I am in great need of confession, so I do hope you have some time later in the week?"

"I always have time, of course, Mrs. Pedigraw. Friday during choir practice would work quite well."

Mrs. Pedigraw had sighed then.

Edward did not want to be alone with the likes of her, and there were many like her. He kept the doors of St. Clement's open to daily groups just for that purpose. The quilters came on Mondays, and he always could count on them to parade in and out of the church, carrying their material and sewing machines to the parish hall. Tuesdays allowed for two grief groups—parents who had lost children and then one for widows and widowers. Wednesdays were full of women praying through the rosary for their sons and husbands who had come home injured from Vietnam. Edward tried to make himself available to those who broke down throughout the day. Those women were genuine. Thursdays were for the building committee, and Fridays were his favorite with choir practice. Saturdays were often busy with weddings or funerals, and confession was only available directly before weekend Mass.

"Father Edward?" A child's voice broke him from his morning reverie, and he jumped. He held his breath and hoped she would go away. Instead, she repeated, "Father Edward?"

Edward quickly dropped his cigarette butt and ground it into the dirt beneath the lilacs with his foot. He looked around, but everything was a blur. He could spot a heaped object on the step below the gate to his neighbors' yard. That must be her, he thought. "Good morning, aren't you up early?"

"I was thinking the same about you. Why are you up so early? And I thought priests weren't supposed to smoke? My mom says that you don't have problems like the rest of us. If that were true, then why are you smoking?"

Edward ignored her questions and asked, "How would your mother know about priests? I don't believe I have seen your family at services?"

Without his glasses, the girl looked like she was sitting on her haunches, and he could hear her digging around with a stick. Her head turned, and Edward imagined her eyes boring into his soul. "My mom knows everything about this town and that old church. She grew up attending St. John's. She said no one at church ever had time for the likes of her—for the families that live in these crackerjack box houses. You still haven't answered my question—why were you smoking?"

Edward avoided the question by walking away and mumbling about his morning calls. He couldn't see but could almost hear the girl's countenance fall. He heard her mother yelling for her from their house. "Margaret, leave the father alone. He isn't concerned about people like us— he is only concerned about those with deep pockets."

Just as Edward reached the front door, it swung open and Alice appeared with what must have been a broom. To Edward, it looked like a scarecrow had emerged from the doorway. "Oh, excuse me, Father Edward, did you take a morning walk? And without your glasses? You should have let me know, and I would have been up to make your coffee. Do give me some warning next time. I don't like feeling like I've been sleeping on the job. Let me get this walkway swept and then I'll have breakfast ready in no time. Do scrambled eggs sound good?"

Any appetite that Edward had was now gone. All he wanted were some quiet moments alone, but it seemed impossible. Breakfast would certainly include listening to Alice talk about Buddy's latest. If her son wasn't starting a new job, he was finding a reason to quit one. "Sometimes I just feel like he was meant for the cloth, don't you agree, Father Edward? Do you think you might be willing to talk to him tonight when he calls? Without a real father, I think he needs some male guidance, and no one could do that better than you."

Edward had barely managed to eat the blurry breakfast and, while choking down the eggs, Alice must have thought he was nodding his consent. "Oh, thank you so much, Father Edward. This would mean the world to me. I could die happy knowing my son was giving his life to the church. Is that how your mother felt?"

"I apologize, Alice. I just remembered that the Johnsons were headed to the hospital early today for Mr.

Johnson's surgery." Edward jumped up and straightened his collar. "I promised I would sit with Mrs. Johnson."

"I didn't see that on your calendar." Alice chastised. "Try to remember to update your calendar each night so I will know best how to serve you."

"Of course, Alice. Thank you for breakfast." Edward mumbled as he wondered how different this was from married life. He thought that by remaining unmarried priests were to live untangled from worldly affairs. This felt like being yoked.

Edward went to his bedroom and shut the door. He immediately dropped to his knees and began prostrations—as quietly as possible. This was all he could do during times of frustration or temptation. "Have mercy on me, God," he repeated. After perhaps twenty, Edward sat on the end of his bed, which Alice must have made during his jaunt outside. He had tried to relieve her of the task of cleaning his room, but she had ignored him.

"Jesus, please help!" Edward muttered. Not very standard, he thought, but this was most often his prayer lately. He grabbed his thick, black-rimmed glasses, put them on, and surveyed the room. It was much like a nun's room, and it probably had been one at some time or another. His cell. A single bed, a nightstand with a lamp, and a small closet. Edward kept a Bible and a few books on a shelf in the nightstand. A rosary was placed neatly on top of the books. He had mainly tossed out everything of a personal nature—too many nosy housekeepers over the years.

Edward jerked open the nightstand drawer and the contents shifted noisily. He took stock of the contents of the drawer—his car keys, a comb, a lone key, a pen, a notebook, some loose change, a stack of pictures held together by a rubber band, and a wallet, made up the bulk of his meager possessions. Two small keepsakes held value for him alone—

a wooden elephant and an obsidian arrowhead. He scooped them up and closed his hand around them.

Chapter 2

Christine just knew, simple as that.

"What were you saying, Chrissy?" her mother, Teresa, asked.

Christine hesitated, searching for the right words. "I said God told me I should talk to Diane."

Teresa stared hard at her for a moment and then turned back to her cooking. "That is interesting, but you really shouldn't say such things. Clairvoyance runs on the French side of our family, but either way, it is dangerous to entertain those thoughts. It could be the devil, and people will think you are odd. Besides, in my opinion, Beverly would be a much more suitable friend. Her mom is in the garden club with me.

I've never met Diane's parents, but I have heard that her dad spends most of his nights at Benny's."

"Ok, Mom, I will try to get to know Beverly. To tell you the truth, I am just so excited for August that I barely have any interest in making new friends. Plus, I will always have Phyllis. Just think, it is our last year together in junior high. Phyllis said I will easily make friends at the boarding school and quickly forget about her. But that would be impossible."

Teresa smiled at her as she threw the carrot peelings into the compost bowl. "It wouldn't hurt to have more pen pals when you first get to Mt. St. Paul's. It can be pretty lonely at a new school where you don't know a soul. At least that is what the boys have said from their experience."

Lonely? I have never been lonely, Christine thought to herself. She watched her mother move briskly, yet gracefully, through her kitchen tasks. Teresa had on her freshly ironed white blouse, which she always wore when it was time for Patrick, Christine's stepfather, to come home from work. Teresa worked hard on her appearance and kept a trim figure, even after eight children. Her own physical fitness tips had recently been published in a newspaper. Things like, "be sure to hold your stomach in while climbing stairs or lifting objects." Teresa's pin curls looked as fresh and bouncy as when she had woken up that morning.

Christine was happy for her mother. Life was, in some ways, easier for her after she married Patrick. They had a housekeeper, Cordelia, who came each Tuesday while the kids were at school. Cordelia was a handsome, buxom black woman with a common-law marriage to a man named Frank. Christine and her siblings weren't sure who worked harder—their mother or Cordelia. They knew that Cordelia appreciated the hearty lunches Teresa made for her each Tuesday and the jars of lard Teresa saved to give to her. Sometimes, in the summer months, Teresa and Cordelia would work together canning jam—most often wild plum from the buckets of plums Teresa had gathered near Davis Creek. "No tame plums for us," Teresa would say. "We like the wild ones here." Teresa and Cordelia would laugh.

After Christine saw that an ember from Cordelia's cigarette had burned a hole in her brand-new white daisy coverlet, it was easy to imagine that Cordelia lounged around in the afternoons while Teresa cleaned. Christine had seen her mom in action many times to know what an energetic housekeeper she was. As Teresa picked up after the children, she would put on whatever she found as she made her way around the house—singing and dancing the whole time. Soon she would be wearing a shirt or two, several hats, and a catcher's mitt, while kicking a basketball around with her. Then she would lovingly return each object to its rightful owner. In contrast, when Cordelia cleaned, the children would have to search for their belongings and would usually find them jammed in the boys' bedroom closet.

Watching her mother with her fresh shirt and bouncy curls, and listening to her talk about the need for friends, Christine thought about her own appearance, and the word disheveled came to mind. She could never match her mother's ability to look perfect. Teresa was a fashion model, after all, rubbing shoulders with the rich and famous, and also worked as a show commentator. "I'll never look that way," Christine thought, "But unlike my mother, I do not fear being lonely."

As Christine set the table with the eight settings for herself and her siblings—her mother and Patrick always ate after the children—she surveyed the dining room that would soon look like a Norman Rockwell painting with cheerful clean faces, a crisp tablecloth, and shiny candlesticks. It wasn't that scene, however, that Christine brought to mind—the one that reminded her that she was never alone. It was just her bedroom, cheerful and tidy. She knew how fortunate she was to have her own bedroom. Even with five brothers and two sisters, her mother had always insisted that Christine have her own room. She wasn't sure why she got that special treatment.

It was a beautiful room in the corner of the house. There wasn't a moment during the day when the sun wouldn't shine in if she let it. All the kids wanted to be in her room. It drew them like a magnet, or rather, maybe it was Christine herself who did.

The older boys often stopped by in the early mornings before school to tell her about their newest sweethearts or which boys at Modoc High they thought she would like after her year at Mt. St. Paul's.

"What is it like, high school?" Christine would ask them in turn.

Francis said it was a real bore.

Joseph, the dark-haired one, loved all the attention from the girls, and their mother's rule, which strictly forbade more than two dates with any one girl, kept him weighing all the possibilities. Teresa didn't share her sons well, and this kept them from getting too serious.

Anthony adored books and learning, science especially.

Samuel was the brother closest in age to Christine and was always so thoughtful toward her. He had just gifted her with her first pair of bobby socks and a five-year diary, saying that she would need them for high school, which, according to him, was "a thrill-a-minute." He loved every part of high school. It was no wonder since he had just been elected, by a landslide, as Student Body President for his upcoming senior year. Samuel would stay in Christine's room the longest of anyone, and she would have to kick him out so that she could get dressed in time for the short walk to school. As Samuel left the room he would say, with a wink, something like, "Wait until you see how Kevin has changed since junior high—he always asks about you."

After school, the little ones would usually run into her room and jump onto the extra bed. That was another question. Why did her mother outfit her room with twin beds when it was just her? She had told Christine it was for when friends stayed overnight, but even that wasn't allowed yet. "After boarding school, you will be allowed to have friends stay overnight occasionally," Teresa would say.

But all of this activity wasn't part of the sweet scene in her mind, the one where she knew she wasn't alone.

What came to mind was her room in the early morning light while she was still lying in her bed—she always kept the same one. It had crossed her mind to switch once in a while, but she never had. The other bed was neatly made, and Christine enjoyed looking at the white daisy pattern on the coverlet. She would make sure to smooth out the wrinkles each night after the last sibling left for their own room. The wallpaper in her room was pale yellow, but it took on a golden sheen when the sun hit it. Each bed had its own nightstand with small lamps with frosted glass. There was only one object that broke the symmetry—a lone crucifix that her mother had centered on the wall above the bed she slept in. Christine wasn't sure where it had come from, but she couldn't remember ever being without it. Everything else Christine owned fit neatly into her closet, and there wasn't any clutter in the room. The feeling of peace in her room was Christine's constant companion. That feeling was only disturbed when her mother came in to analyze her wardrobe.

Teresa insisted they go through Christine's closet three times a year. The closet clean-outs always coincided with their shopping trips to Delta City. Just like clockwork, Teresa would eyeball Christine and say, "Oh, look, Chrissy, your dress hem is up. You know what they say—a turned-up hem means a new dress is on the way!" Christine had developed the nervous habit of straightening her hem often just for that reason. Once her mother said those words, Christine knew that Teresa had a shopping trip in the works. The shopping trips were a great embarrassment to Christine. She and her brothers were the only ones in Alturas with new clothes from Neiman Marcus every season, or who even traveled out of town to shop. At least her brothers blended in ok with khaki pants and polo shirts, but all the new styles for the girls in the early '60s seemed outlandish.

For this reason and more, Christine's thirteenth birthday party had been a nightmare, mainly because Christine didn't want anyone to see her new "Mamie Eisenhower" pixie haircut. Her mother was obsessed with bangs and would regularly trim Christine's bangs herself. With the new haircut, her bangs were cut nearly to her hairline. The morning of her birthday, Teresa had sent Christine on a dump run with Samuel, and Christine sank into the seat so no one would see her.

Already in a bad mood, Christine came home from the dump to find seven of her friends at her dining room table as a surprise for her birthday. They were seated, prim and proper, as quietly as if in a library. Christine was mortified, and it had gotten worse when her mother made her go into her room to change into the newest dress. The dress was a black chemise with a broad white collar and a bright red bow at the neck. Starting at her hips, the bright red plaid skirt with narrow pleats went to her knees. She wanted to lie down on her bed and die rather than go out in front of the expectant crowd.

The nightmare had continued when her mother said, "Where is the birthday girl? She's a teenager now! Can you believe it, girls?"

Christine knew that most of those girls were just there hoping for a glimpse of one of her handsome older brothers, whose new clothes only made them look even better, while her new dresses and hairstyle just made her look like a clown. Only Phyllis was genuine, understood her situation, and, thankfully, despite her long-time crush on Anthony, was a true bosom friend. Phyllis would always call before coming over—first to see if Anthony was home and secondly to see if they had any of Teresa's famous brownies. Christine knew that Phyllis was holding back her giggles while the other girls only feigned interest in the birthday party. Christine could look forward to laughing about it later with Phyllis if she could survive the rest of the day first.

One thing happened, not long before, that made the thought of wearing the dress slightly more positive—Teresa had finally let Christine shave her legs. It had been awful for Phyllis and Christine, the only girls in their class who weren't allowed to shave their legs. Then the dreadful day came when Phyllis proudly stuck her smooth, hairless legs out in the aisle at school. Christine, mortified, went directly home after school to speak to her mother about it. Teresa was always sunbathing at that time, and Christine remembers finding it easier to ask about shaving while her mother's eyes were closed, head on her arms—the top of her suit loosened to expose her back.

"Mom? Phyllis's mom finally let her shave her legs. May I?" Christine blurted out.

"No," Teresa answered immediately. Then Teresa opened one eye, smiled up at Christine, and then broke out into her favorite Doris Day song—

"When I was just a little girl, I asked my mother what will I be? Will I be pretty? Will I be rich? Here's what she said to me—Que sera, sera. Whatever will be, will be. The future's not ours to see. Que sera, sera. What will be, will be."

Christine ran into the house, dejected. She saw that Anthony and Joseph had overheard the conversation, and then headed outside to talk with Teresa. Christine could hear their low voices, and then they came back inside, triumphant grins on their faces. Joseph said, "Mom said you could shave, Chrissy!" Christine hugged both brothers and immediately ran into the bathroom. She dragged one of her brother's razors over her dry legs, which she would later regret. "At least I won't have to wear the horrid dress with hairy legs," Christine had thought.

"Chrissy?" Teresa opened the door the day of the party and came into her room to fetch her. She put her hands over her mouth in delight and said, "You look like you have just stepped out of the latest magazine. Don't you love it?"
"Oh, yes. Thank you, Mom." Christine could not hurt her mother by saying anything different. Dressing Christine up like a doll seemed to be one of Teresa's greatest pleasures.
Christine can barely remember the horror of the rest of the day. From then on, the thought of surprise parties only filled her with dread, and for the rest of the season, every time her mother made her wear that dress, she took a long camel coat to wear over it at school.

It must have been Teresa's vanity, carried over from her time on the runway, that made her so dead set on the newest fashions. Or maybe it was coming from a large family during the Depression that had fueled Teresa's love of material things. Christine just knew that it was simplicity and cleanliness that she herself loved. The sight of her open closet and all of those clothes made her feel anxious, and she much preferred her tidy scene with the closet door closed.

Christine thought again of the soft, morning light hitting the wallpaper and then gradually fanning out over the empty bed as she lay tucked within her own cool sheets. She could hear the muffled sounds of her mother and stepfather moving around the house, along with her siblings' voices as they woke. One of her brothers let out a hearty laugh, and it made her smile. She was glad she couldn't make out any of their words—the muffled sounds were soothing. The only words she could make out were the ones that were repeating softly in her own mind, "God is wherever you let God in."

She couldn't think of where she had heard those words. Every week at Mass, she would listen carefully to see if they were repeated among the responsive readings or in the hymns. She had many favorite phrases there, too, like "Lord, make me an instrument of your peace," but it was those other words that would come over her like a soft breeze.

Christine repeated those words to herself that evening as she finished setting the table—"God is wherever you let God in," and she smiled to herself. That is what it is, she thought, my room is full of God. He comes in with the sunlight more and more each day and has never left. There was always room for more. Maybe God wants me to share some of that light with Diane.

"Why are you smiling?" her mother asked her.

Christine knew that her thoughts wouldn't be received the way she wanted and that would make her anxious later, so she just said, "I'm just wondering what the boys will talk about when they get home from practice today."

Teresa flashed her coquettish, beautiful smile then and replied, "It will be entertaining, no doubt. The table looks beautiful, Dear. Thank you. You are off the hook for dishes tonight."

Christine answered, "Oh, I don't mind, Mom. Samuel and I have so much fun doing the dishes together." She smiled to herself, then, when she thought about the candy Samuel would surely bribe her with.

"Please help me do the dishes tonight, Chrissy?" He never failed to ask. "I have York Peppermint Patties this time." Then he whispered, "I went to that old forbidden bowling alley just to buy them special for you. I can't wait to tell you about what happened in Mr. Nelson's class this morning."

Christine knew that Samuel just wanted her with him. He would end up doing most of the work while he talked anyway. Elbow-deep in dishwater, he would scrub and talk while Christine gave him her undivided attention—slowly drying each dish.

Chapter 3

The wooden elephant was the only item Edward could call his own as a child, and that was because he kept it hidden. It felt like his parents had long ago folded themselves up and tucked themselves neatly away—like in a file folder. His older siblings looked at Edward as if he were a replacement brother who had fallen short of their expectations. Or like he, too, might not reach adulthood, so don't waste your time becoming attached. The younger siblings treated him exactly like their parents wanted them to—as one earmarked for the priesthood. You don't beg your older brother to play cops and robbers when he has been dedicated to God.

Edward's childhood home was like a museum. His grandparents had come to America with work ethic, talent, and intelligence, and their status in the church was their first concern. Their house, built by their grandfather, Luke, was well admired by all. Edward and his siblings and cousins called him "Grosspapa," and their Grosspapa had built many of the churches in their city and was the German of all Germans in the town. Edward's grandfather had built their parish church, and its beauty, complete with stained-glass windows brought over from the fatherland, rivaled any other church in the country. His family lived and breathed the Catholic Church as if stopping the connection would be like suffocating. From what he was told, everything was magnified after the accident.

Outside the stuffy walls of his house, Edward had just one ally—his cousin, Eugenia. Gigi, as he liked to call her, was a few years older and had appointed herself the family historian. She was the fifth of eight children, and her mother had barely survived an illness to give birth to her. Gigi would whisper to Edward, "She didn't even breastfeed me—she was so sick. It's no wonder she got pregnant again so soon, not nursing me and all. I am not exaggerating when I say it's almost like I didn't exist. I got left behind on Sundays more than once."

Edward often felt left behind when he listened to Gigi talk. What does breastfeeding have to do with having another baby?

Gigi's parents had gotten right down to business by dedicating their first son to God's service. All in all, she told Edward, their grandparents' family had at least five priests and seven nuns in their lineage. More precisely, she would say, "We have twelve religious in our family. I don't know what our forebears did wrong, but Grosspapa seems hell-bent on trying to make up for it," Gigi told him.

Her word choices always gave Edward a lot to think about. He had no idea what their forebears' sins were, but he was starting to get a sense of his own family.

No one in town could outshine their family's contribution to the Catholic Church. Grandfather building other churches was one thing, but then he went and donated his own prized house to be used as the rectory, choosing a more modest dwelling for himself and their grandmother. This was after the accident, after Edward's brother's body had been laid in the house for the mourners to pay their respects. Donating the house seemed like a bargain with God, and his mother, pregnant with him at the time, had gone ahead and thrown Edward in with the bargain.

People worshipped their grandfather. Gigi and Edward could not deny his talent as a craftsman every Sunday, as they stared up at the intricacies of the ceiling and admired the lights embedded throughout the altar. Looking back, Edward wondered why he hadn't felt pride in his grandfather's accomplishments—he had only felt dread, like a weight upon his shoulders. He was expected to grow up and pay a debt he knew nothing about.

At parish picnics, Gigi would do her best to try to draw Edward into the games. Just when Edward thought he could escape and join her, he would hear his mother say, "Edward, would you please join me in welcoming the Cunninghams to our community? Eugenia, please come as well, and maybe you can invite their children to play?"

Gigi would take the children to play, but Edward's mother would hold onto his arm as she made adult conversation. She was priming him for the church, and he knew it. "Edward, would you please go and refill their glasses? Edward, would you please explain all the classes we have for their children at the church? Edward would be happy to give you a tour of the church square. Our Edward, do you know that he memorized the Nicene Creed when he was just three years old? I don't want to assume to know the Lord's intentions, but Edward seems to have His anointing on his life."

Even at his young age, Edward tried to practice pre-forgiveness with his mother. From what Gigi had told him, there had been a drastic change in her after the accident, and it was no wonder. He couldn't understand why she was so animated around others but withdrawn at home. As uncomfortable as he was playing a child priest to her friends, he never felt more loved by his mother than in those moments, and he craved her love more than anything.

His earliest memories of her at home were all the same. She would be sitting in her chair, staring out the window, with the wooden elephant in her hand. She would worry her fingers over the elephant while she looked out at their backyard. If he had been in her lap at the time, it was like her distraction was gradually nudging him off. He would eventually drop to the floor in search of something to do.

"Stay close, Edward," she would say while her gaze was averted. He would do just as he was told and pull the box of toys out from beneath the couch.

"Mother?" he would say, pushing his glasses back into place. "Here are the other animals. May I have that one?"

She wouldn't answer, but she kept fingering the elephant. Edward would silently line up the other animals from the wooden ark and retell the story to himself. Everything was in order, except for a lone elephant among the other pairs, marching with their orders from God. For as long as he could remember, Edward always felt safest when everything was in order. He had heard people say that he was an "obsessive child." He wasn't sure what that meant, but he did like his room to be tidy and everything "just so." After telling the story with the wooden ark, he would line up all the animals again and feel anxious about the missing elephant.

One day, the scene played out as before, but this time his mother had his baby sister on her lap—even farther removed from Edward. She had put the casserole in the oven before giving his sister the bottle. After the accident, his mother hadn't nursed any of them, according to Gigi. So little Eleanor was lying there on their mother's lap—the bottle had long been drained of its contents, and Eleanor had turned her head to watch Edward. Her mouth was slack with a drop of milk about to fall when the fire alarm sounded. Everyone startled, but his mother did most of all. She ran to the kitchen with Eleanor still clutched to her. The bottle dropped from Eleanor's mouth just as the elephant dropped from his mother's hand.

Edward sat in his spot and waited. He looked from the dropped elephant back to the lone elephant marching ahead. If the pair didn't board the ark, how would their kind reproduce and fill the earth post-flood? Wasn't that the Lord's command for everyone? "Be fruitful and multiply. Fill the earth?" He could hear his mother exclaiming over the burned casserole and calling for his older sister to grab the baby. Quick as a flash, Edward ran across the floor and grabbed the elephant. He considered putting it back with the others, but then thought better of it. He crept off to the room he shared with his brother and put the elephant under a loose floorboard he had discovered.

Edward was surprised by himself for doing something outside the glass box his parents had put him in. On the one hand, he felt emboldened—on the other, he felt guilty for stealing something so important to his mother. He could hear her countless prayers to St. Anthony about the elephant—St. Anthony had never failed her before. Why now?

Edward didn't even know why she liked the elephant so much, but maybe he would feel something when he held it. Perhaps he would feel close to his mother by holding it close? Often, after a long day at school, Edward would run upstairs to check on the elephant. The rest of the siblings would gather over snacks in the kitchen, while Edward would wonder what kind of magic the elephant held.

Edward and his siblings attended St. Benedict's parish school, along with Gigi and all the multitude of cousins and second-cousins-once-removed. There would have been even more cousins if so many had not been called to be "religious," but their numbers were still pretty high, given that their grandparents had had ten children. Edward would hear his older siblings complain that they would never find someone to marry, since they were related to everyone at the school. "That is what summer camp is for," Mother would reply.

Every summer, all the parishes in the diocese would petition to send their youth to Emerald City for camp. No one would need to petition Edward's family. They had donated their property to be used as a summer camp after his brother had died there. Edward would often wonder how his parents could stand to send their kids there after the tragedy, but every year it was the same thing—two weeks before school ended, parents would rush to make sure there was still room for their children to attend. His parents didn't really need to rush, however. Most likely, that had been part of the agreement when they donated the property—their names at the top of the list, everyone's but Edward's. Edward didn't need to do what other children did. Edward didn't need to find a future spouse. Edward couldn't be trusted at the water's edge. Edward needed to learn how to be an altar boy. Edward was destined for the priesthood. Besides, Edward was shy and had poor eyesight.

The first summer the reality sank in, Edward watched his family as if from the outside. Edward's older brother gave him what was meant to be a comforting whack on his back as he went out the door with his duffel bag and sporting equipment banging against the doorframe. Edward had to push his glasses back up on his nose, and then he watched his three older sisters ignore him as they walked by, talking between themselves about which boys they hoped to see again. Of course, he still had his little sister, Eleanor, faithful to her core. She snuck up behind and grabbed his hand. "It's ok, Edward. We will sneak in lots of radio time and popcorn after you are done at the church."

Chapter 4

Christine felt her stepfather, Patrick, growing even more distant as the time approached for her to leave for Mt. St. Paul's. He had paid for each of her older brothers' freshman year at prestigious boarding schools, but Christine had heard the heated arguments at night as Patrick refused to pay for her.

"She always has her head in the clouds and doesn't need the same education as the boys. She has her good looks, that's all she will need in life," Patrick had said over too many bourbons.

One day, Teresa came home in a flourish, swinging her purse and dancing into the room. She said that a miracle had taken place. "I have the money for you to go to Mt. St. Paul's! It's truly a miracle. There is even enough money left over for some of your necessities. We need to give thanks to the Mother of God for her prayers for you."

Teresa was a long-time representative for the Miraculous Medal Association, whose aim was to inspire devotion to Mary. Teresa was diligent in setting aside one hour each afternoon at her desk in the corner of the kitchen to type the cards and address the association envelopes. The association had to be the longest-running association in the world—it even predated Vatican I. "I signed up for the association when I was pregnant with you and was still very active in the Holy Family Catholic Church's Mothers' Club. You were a miracle, after all, thanks be to our Blessed Mother. You were Murph's final good deed before he was gone. I really didn't think I would have any more children after Samuel, since we both nearly died at his birth. It took me years to recover."

Christine cringed. It reminded her of when she had learned about the birds and the bees at the same time that Teresa was big and pregnant with Maggie. Christine had been the only girl her age with a pregnant mother, and it mortified her to realize all of the finer details involved.

Christine knew better than to ask questions of her mother about the money for school, but she made sure to thank God in her prayers. She also asked Mother Mary to continue to pray for all of them. It was so comforting to imagine such a pure, heavenly mother watching out for her. She sometimes felt that Teresa was a touch too scandalous.

Christine's main prayers lately had also focused on her younger siblings. She was so concerned about what it would be like for them when she was gone. There would be no more late-night or early-morning snuggles in her bedroom. It seemed like the three younger children had yo-yoed between being spoiled and yet neglected. Somewhere in the middle would have been more stable for them.

Her three youngest siblings, Patrick Jr., Abigail, and Maggie (short for Margaret), were actually her half-siblings—Teresa's children by Patrick. Patrick had Teresa change the last names of her first five children to Harrison without legally adopting them. He wanted all the glory for eight children but not the legal responsibility for the first five. Christine knew the oldest brothers were especially a status symbol for him, and the youngest were as darling as could be. How come Patrick didn't seem to have any pride where she herself was concerned?

"It is actually you and me both," Samuel explained during a long afternoon together. They had ended up in Christine's bedroom, and Samuel lay on the other twin bed as they talked. "There are the older three and the younger three, which leaves you and me in the middle. He only cares about the older boys and his own kids. The older boys are smart and funny, and they love to hunt. Old Pat brags about all the birds they shoot and then sends me out in the snow to clean them over the garbage can. Pretty soon, I am freezing and wet and covered in feathers—the colder my hands get, the colder my heart grows towards him. His latest sick game is to promise to help me shoot my first buck, but then he uses me to flush the deer out of the aspen stands—he shoots the buck before I even get a chance."

"That's awful," Christine said. "I don't remember those early years, so I am glad you are sharing."

"I guess you and I were the bad part of the bargain," Samuel speculated. "For Old Pat, it was like our mother and brothers just emerged, fairy-like, from the woods, where we were living. He probably had caught wind of the outdoorswoman and fashion model living off the land with her strapping sons, and knew they would help his prospects for being elected district attorney. Did you know Mom only dated him for two weeks before agreeing to marry him? I could punch Francis now. Mom asked him for his advice, and he told her it was a good idea to marry him. I don't get it. Our lives were perfect without a stepdad."

"I remember the story now. Didn't Patrick have a fancy car with electric windows? He would let you boys roll them up and down over and over."

"That's right. That's all it took for Francis and the others. They were starved for a father figure. Francis was like a dad to you and me, so we did not need anyone else."

"But didn't you like those electric windows, too?"

Samuel looked ashamed and admitted that he had. "Yes. Do you remember how they left us with that ranching family while they went on their honeymoon?" Samuel sat up on the bed and looked over at the crucifix above Christine's bed. "I am not sure why I remember this, but I remember Mom leaving that crucifix in the room we stayed in at that ranch. She carted that thing everywhere, even in our tent when we camped. I am not sure why it always hangs in your room. The rest of us don't have one. I wouldn't want one, anyway."

"That's true," Christine said. "I never noticed that before—that I am the only one with a crucifix. Now, what were you saying about their honeymoon?"

"Oh, yeah, well, as soon as they came back and loaded us all up in the car, Old Pathetic Pat whipped his head around and yelled at us to 'never touch the window controls again.' I'll never forget the first time seeing that cruel look in his eyes and, in that moment, I would have given anything to jump out and run back to our old camp."

From her brothers' memories, Christine had formed her own idyllic images of what those early years before Patrick had been like—living in their charming house a short walk from the Holy Family Catholic Church. She obviously had no memories of her real parents' tumultuous marriage before her birth. Her mother had kicked her father out while still pregnant with her.

Samuel had told her sad stories about their real father. Murph was all Irish, and his family had immigrated to Illinois from "the Old Sod" the generation before. Murph's mother, Nora, their grandmother, was a strong, intelligent woman. Nora had been a beloved schoolteacher before she married. When the Depression hit, it must have pushed Murph's father into what his mother called "melancholy or shock." One evening, he had walked up the aisle of the Catholic Church and shot himself in front of the altar. That was a terrible scandal for a Catholic family in those days.

"Grandmother Nora took Murph into her room the next day and told him that his father had died of shock," Samuel said in a dramatic voice. It was the most tragic thing Christine had ever heard.

Samuel continued, "It is no wonder Murph became an alcoholic. After his mother took bag and baggage and moved her family out to Berkeley, poor Murph had to help pay his brother's way through medical school. He and his brother used to have horrible fist fights over it. Another brother became a renowned engineer, and his younger sister was, of course, doted on. Murph felt used, I'm sure. Then our own mother kept up the whole song and dance. She once told us she had only married Murph for his convertible. In fact, maybe she only married Patrick for his car, too."

Christine didn't know what to say. It was horrible to think of their flesh and blood with all these problems. Finally, she asked, "Do you think Mom is really that shallow?"

"Is the Pope Catholic?" Samuel responded. Then he added, "No, I am only joking, I am sure the hard circumstances drove her to it, and she was just making light of it. I guess Murph told Mom that if she didn't marry him, he would start drinking and never stop. She thought he must really love her."

Before the separation, it was evident that the drinking had gotten the best of Murph anyway, and the boys started finding him passed out on the floor. Things had definitely been more peaceful in their new house once Murph had moved out, and they only saw him sporadically. The new location was perfect for the boys, both for their duties as altar servers and for continuing their studies at the parish school. Peace prevailed in their home with no more explosive episodes between their parents. Their mother's energy and joy were magnified without all the contention as she recovered from Samuel's birth.

When Teresa's pregnancy with Christine became apparent, her fashion show contacts asked her to commentate rather than model. This was a huge compliment, given that Teresa had never been formally trained, and it also brought in more money. Murph had been irregular with his child support payments, so any extra money was welcome. Her wit and humor were well known, and they came in handy both on the microphone and in the evenings at home with the children. The older boys were well on their way to developing that same humor and charm, and their nights around board games were lively and full of laughter. Teresa would tease the boys before bedtime with the question, "Who loves Mother best?" Then, once they were in their pajamas, she would recite the Joy Allison poem with a twinkle in her eye:

> "'I love you, Mother,' said little John,
> Then, forgetting his work, his cap went on;
> And he was off to the garden swing,
> And she had the wood and water to bring.

'I love you, Mother,' said rosy Nell,
'I love you more than tongue can tell.'
Then she teased and pouted half the day,
Till her mother was glad when she went to play.

'I love you, Mother,' said little Fan,
'Today I'll help you all I can.
How glad I am school doesn't keep!'
Then she rocked the baby till it went to sleep.

And stepping softly she brought the broom,
And swept the floor and tidied the room.
Busy and happy all day was she.
Helpful and happy as child could be.

'I love you, Mother,' again they said—
Three little children going to bed.
How do you think that mother guessed
Which of them really loved her best?'"

When she finished reciting, the boys would crowd around, hug Teresa, and say, "I love you, Mother," repeatedly until Teresa would say, "Ok, Ok, you all love me equally, and, so that you know, you are all my favorites."

Christine was born into this cheerful atmosphere on a chilly January morning. She was the only child born in the winter, as Teresa usually tried to have her children in the warmer months. Christine was the instant pride and joy of the entire family, and she was never without a set of arms to carry her around and to keep her bundled and warm. Christine's arrival had ushered in a new beginning for all of them, and even Samuel finally felt at ease.

This was the rhythm that flowed for the first few years of Christine's life. When school let out for the summer, Teresa would drive them to Cedarville, five hours north of Delta City, where she fostered relationships with local ranching families. The area reminded Teresa of her childhood in Wyoming, with mountains rising dramatically from valleys dotted with ranches and farms.

Teresa loved exploring, both alone and with the children. As a child, Teresa had been praised for her keen eyes and adventurous spirit. She had once found a prairie hen nest with ten eggs, and her mother had said, "Oh, you little sharp eyes." It was the only praise she ever remembered receiving from her overworked mother, and that phrase had become a source of pride for Teresa. She later gave Abigail the nickname because she took after her mother with her sharp eyes.

Teresa loved hunting and hiking, and she was intentional about maintaining her figure. She would strap Christine to her back and take off in the early mornings with her .22 caliber rifle or 30-30 Winchester. Ground squirrels were a pest to local ranchers, and Teresa kept a running tally of how many she eliminated.

Her friends lent Teresa their camping gear, and sometimes she would camp for weeks at a time with the children. She believed the outdoors promoted her children's good health, and Christine was thriving with the lifestyle. Occasionally, Teresa would leave her children with a friend and make the drive to Delta City for a fashion show. When the fruit trees would ripen toward the end of summer, Teresa would can the fruit. One summer, she had to rent a small trailer to take no less than 400 jars of fruit back to the valley. She didn't mind letting it slip just how many jars she had canned while attending some of the church functions in Delta City. Teresa was very competitive.

The church had done her duty in helping the beautiful young family in those months following the divorce and Christine's birth, but even goodwill can give way to human faults such as jealousy and resentment. The married women of the parish soon grew tired of this energetic and beautiful single mother in their midst. The more tightly they held on to their husbands, the less they were able to open their arms to Teresa and her children. They no longer needed Teresa's help in the Mother's Club or candy sales committee. The boys weren't invited to stay overnight any longer. Even their intelligence and good looks were resented by the insecure mothers.

They wondered how Teresa managed to keep her trim figure with five children and to undertake massive house projects. Even while nearly eight months pregnant, she had managed to get a life-sized plaster-of-Paris manger scene onto the roof in time for Christmas—winning the blue ribbon in the neighborhood Christmas decoration contest. And how did she manage to have impeccable hair and clothing, and didn't she just volunteer with Gregory Peck at an American Cancer Society event? It was all too much for those women.

Teresa had felt the air grow cold among the parishioners even as the spring air grew warmer outside, and she would not allow her children to be stifled in those conditions. One day, the children woke up to boxes, and it was apparent Teresa had spent the whole night packing.

"We are moving to the mountains," she informed them.

The older boys, who couldn't believe their ears, whooped and hollered and slapped each other on the back.

"Can we bring Chrissy?" Samuel asked with great concern.

"Jesus, Mary, and Joseph!" Teresa exclaimed. "Of course, Samuel, don't be a worry-wart. By hook or crook, we will even bring the chickens."

Chapter 5

Edward hadn't gone looking for a hideaway that first time—it was more like he had been driven there.

It was an early winter morning, and Edward was smoking his cigarette in the dark. He was enjoying the smell of burning wood from other early risers who were starting their mornings by lighting fires. Wood stoves were new to him when he first moved to the West as a missionary priest. Back in Ohio, they used radiators and coal stoves for heat. He was just about to finish his smoke when Alice rushed out the back door looking for him. He moved in closer to the lilac.

Edward wasn't sure why his admiration for wine was ok with the church while cigarettes were strictly forbidden. As long as he could remember, he had heard church members laugh about wine and how "we do love the Precious Blood, after all." It's not that he was happy about his smoking or drinking—he was planning to cut way back soon, but he just wondered why smoking was worse than the other vice. Cutting back to two a day couldn't be attributed to self-control on Edward's part—it was more his inability to get away from the watchful eyes of Alice. He knew full well that the diocese had hired Alice for her reputation for tenacity and the eyes she had in the back of her head. The parish apparently couldn't afford to give Edward too much independence, and, with Alice around, they made sure he couldn't catch a moment to himself.

"Father Edward? Father Edward? Are you out here? We had a call that the pipes burst in the parish hall."

From his spot near the lilac and the rubbish bins, Edward could see Alice on the back step in her bathrobe, squinting under the glare of the lightbulb. Even with his glasses this time, she somehow resembled a scarecrow. "Father Edward? Are you finished with the cats? It's freezing out here. Are you alright? It's the pipes in the parish hall—they have burst." Edward had told Alice that he likes to feed the feral cats early in the morning, so she keeps him well-stocked with outdated milk, cat food, and pie tins left over from the parish suppers.

"Father Edward? I think the water has already reached the carpets in the foyer."

Edward ground the last of his cigarette into the dirt around the light post and then continued into the shadows of the back alley. Plumbing was not a part of his job description.

Edward knew he had an 8:00 appointment with Earl, but with dementia, Earl would more than likely be a no-show.

In fact, Earl is the one they would call about the pipes, so this could work well. Earl was still the most knowledgeable plumber in town, even if he regularly walked out of his house with no pants. Edward missed Earl's wife, Rose, almost as much as Earl did, but he couldn't help but be envious of Earl's independence.

From the alley, Edward turned right and hurried past the row of houses on Church St. He hoped his parishioners were busy feeding their own cats or removing their curlers. Houses were set further back once he made the right turn onto Pine Blvd., and Edward's mind started to clear up. He quickened his pace and crossed the street, hoping he would blend in with the concrete wall. It was getting light out, and he was sure to draw unwelcome attention. His glasses always slipped down his face when he was nervous, and that morning, they were quite an annoyance. His doctor had just informed him that his macular degeneration was progressing and had changed his prescription. Maybe he would finally get a pair of glasses that fit correctly. His mother was nearly blind from her macular degeneration by the time she passed. Smoking was probably not helping, nor were his other habits.

This was a new sensation for Edward—that of being free and alone—and it felt exhilarating. As a child, he had loved his siblings and, of course, Gigi, but rarely had a moment to himself. His whole life, he had felt like he was on display and smothered. His mother could somehow ignore him while simultaneously keeping him in her sight. In her mind, it would only take one moment alone for him to suffer the same fate as George.

Edward inhaled the cool morning air and quickened his pace. He started to run, but then slowed when he knew he would draw attention to himself. Long strides were nearly as rewarding. This could be his new hobby.

Driven along by Alice's voice ringing in his ears, Edward now found himself at the entrance to the old mining site. He had never been there but had heard about the wooden bridges and rushing stream that filled the draw below the mining relics. He and Gigi had a similar creekside hiding spot back in Ohio. They would escape there during large family gatherings. Of course, Gigi was the one who thought of the name for their hideout—Muk's Ruk. It made no sense at all, but that was what made it so fun.

He could write her a letter and ask for her reasoning behind the name. She could help him come up with a name for his new escape. Was he surprised that she had become religious as well? He was. Gigi was a Sister of the Precious Blood and spent her days in academia and research. Maybe she had entered the religious life to feel closer to Edward. Edward remembered a day when their religious aunts had asked Gigi if she was going to take vows. Edward smiled, remembering Gigi's answer.

"Isn't it a bit soon to tell?" she had said with spunk. "I haven't even made up my mind if I like boys yet!"

Edward grabbed a spare cigarette from his pocket—allowing himself this extra since his other smoke had been cut short prematurely. He wanted to sit and enjoy the sound of the rushing stream and perhaps pray. Was it wrong to pray while he was smoking?

The truth was that he felt adrift, and prayer had become difficult.

What was he even doing with his life? Was he making a difference for anyone, or helping anyone?

Maybe this was the season he had been warned about—the dark night of the soul.

St. John of the Cross had penned those words as the title of a poem.

At the seminary, the professors had warned the seminarians about a time that would come for all those of faith, especially the religious. It was imperative not to fall into despair when one felt like a failure.

A time of disillusionment.

Who am I even kidding? Edward thought.

What did any of it matter? I drink, I smoke, I hide from the women in the parish. I lie about my appointments.

A word came to Edward then—Dochero.

"What in the world is a Dochero?" Edward whispered, and he felt the chill that comes right at sunrise.

A voice broke the silence. "What did you say?"

It was the girl from behind the parsonage.

"Did you follow me?" Edward asked, jumping up and dropping his cigarette in the stream.

"I was about to ask you the same thing. I was here first. This is my spot."

"What is a girl your age doing way out here before the sun is even up? It is not safe."

"My name is Margaret, and I don't know why I first ended up here. Maybe because it is peaceful here. Better than all the yelling at the house. Why are you here? Looking for a place to sneak your smokes?"

"I'm not sure. I guess I was curious. It's nice here. But I'd best get back now." Edward brushed off his pants and started up the hill.

"What was that word you said?" Margaret asked. "Dough something?"

Edward hesitated, feeling a bit foolish. He wasn't a kid anymore, and he surely shouldn't be here talking to one. "It was nothing."

"Oh." The girl looked crestfallen, and Edward hurried away.

Well, that had been nice while it lasted, Edward thought. But then she was there. He would have to come back during school hours. Surely Margaret went to school?

Edward said Dochero to himself again, then decided to find a place to sit, hidden behind the old mining equipment. He didn't want to leave just yet.

Edward knew it then, why he had enjoyed that brief moment of nothing but the stream and the trees. The feeling was similar to what he had experienced for as long as he remembered—during the liturgy at Mass. Despite all the distractions of his childhood—the fuss around his family's wealth and notoriety, their involvement in the church, the mounting pressure for him to go to seminary, getting the large family to church on time—everything faded during the liturgy. Gigi had been the one to tell him that the liturgy was when they could worship God with the angels and the saints. It was when they could leave behind all earthly cares and enter into the mystery.

She had said, "Grosspapa designed that apse with every attention to detail that he could muster. Isn't it gorgeous? He wanted people to realize they are among the heavenly when they come to worship God here. Look around you, though, most people have their heads in the sand. They are too distracted to enter the holy. I should stop talking now. We need to focus on worship."

And Edward decided to focus with every ounce of his being. He believed Gigi and wanted to enter that worship. He asked God to let him enter, and he imagined himself standing before the throne—surrounded by heroes like Peter and Elijah, worshipping God. He wasn't sure if it was right, but he imagined his brother, George, there. He asked God to forgive him if that was wrong.

The family talked about George so much that he had become a hero in Edward's mind. George had been his older brother after all. Besides being full of life as a five-year-old, everyone said that George spoke of the things of God as one much wiser than his years.

The day of the accident, George had been waiting for their father to come pick him up from his grandparents' house. The family's house in Emerald City was right on the edge of Silver Lake, with its own dock. Since the family didn't speak openly of the details, Edward learned most of this information from the newspaper clipping hidden deep in a drawer. The clipping said that George had drowned in eight feet of water.

If Edward thought long enough, he knew that he was guilty of George's death by his own existence. Edward's mother had suffered from debilitating morning sickness while pregnant with him. She had sent the active George away to stay with his grandparents at their summer house for ten days because of her illness. Edward felt sick, too, just thinking about it. Ten days is a long time for a little one to be away from his mother, father, and siblings.

That fateful morning, George knew his father was finally coming to take him home. He ran out to the pier to wait for his father's boat. The grandparents assumed he had gone to church with other family members. This was another example of how their whole lives centered on the church—and, when Edward was younger, if he wasn't blaming the accident on himself, he was blaming the church. Their grandparents had already taken George to Saturday Mass, so they weren't attending that fateful Sunday. They assumed George had been anxious to go with his cousins while they enjoyed a leisurely morning at home. They had watched from their windows as everyone loaded into the car. They apparently had not counted the number of children.

While his aunt, uncle, and cousins loaded up into the car, George yelled to Thomas, his favorite cousin and Gigi's brother, that he wanted to stay behind to watch for his father's boat. Thomas had answered George with a hearty wave and smile. Of course, it was Gigi who told Edward all of those details.

George must have gone right to the edge of the pier and strained against the railing to look for the boat carrying his father. He must have grown weary of the wait, not even considering the danger, or maybe he had spotted something in the water and then looked down, falling in.

It was only when their father arrived and the others came back from church that the family realized George was missing. It was hours before someone in the family even thought to look in the water.

As a child, Edward had imagined a boy, looking much like himself, floating angelically just beneath the surface of the water. Why did the image seem so peaceful to him? Born of a womb and then returning to a watery womb. Had the boys shared some sort of connection then, since Edward himself was safe in their mother's womb at that time?

Edward jumped up abruptly and shook off the thoughts. I am adrift, he thought again.

Edward forced himself to make the walk back to the church and back to Alice's clutches. Dochero would have to wait. No doubt Alice had already alerted Bishop James about the burst pipes and that Edward had gone missing in their time of need. Bishop James was probably already on his way. Yet another trip over from the diocese in the valley to investigate. It was no secret that Edward was under close watch.

Chapter 6

"Chrissy, has anyone ever told you that you are a good listener?" Teresa turned down the radio and Christine's favorite, Gene Autry, before glancing over at Christine sitting in the passenger seat on their drive down to Mt. St. Paul's.

"Yes, you have told me that before," Christine responded, happily working her way through a big bag of Fritos.

"Well, you do have quite the gift for listening. You should always remember that and be sure to use it down there among all of those girls."

It was true that Christine liked to listen. She was accustomed to listening to all of her mother's stories and her siblings' stories—quite content to just stand or sit alongside them as they talked. Her mind would sometimes wander as she imagined the events of their tales. Sometimes she would even write about them in her diary.

It was a little more challenging to listen that day as they made the trip to Mt. St. Paul's. It was the biggest day of her life thus far. At first, she had been sad to leave all her siblings behind when Teresa announced she wanted to make the trip alone with Christine.

"This is her day," Teresa had explained to the others. "Chrissy has rarely had a moment alone with me her whole life, and it's time."

Nobody ever argued with Teresa, unless you counted what happened with Patrick when all the kids went to bed.

The summer had passed quickly for Christine. Between the social comings and goings of her older brothers and her days watching the younger three, there hadn't been much of a chance for boredom. Christine would often walk Pat Jr., Abigail, and Maggie to the public pool and then stop at the store for ice cream on their way back.

"There's Putt Putt, kids. Wave at him." Christine would say when they would catch a glimpse of one of the town's local personalities.

On one of those occasions, Maggie wrinkled up her face and said, "I don't know why you always talk about him and wave at him. He is so weird. Aren't we supposed to stay clear of strangers?"

"It's not his fault he is that way," Christine answered. "It doesn't cost us anything to wave and smile. He can't hurt us, and besides, he isn't a stranger.. He is a friend of our town—he watches over us."

Putt Putt's real name was Alfred, and, with his pale blue captain's hat and blue and white checked shirt as a uniform, he considered himself to be the security patrol for their town. He rode his bike all day up and down the side streets. When he needed to rest, he would park on the corners and face Main Street with one foot resting on the curb. His sister, Nelda, was in Christine's class, so Putt Putt wasn't too far from Christine's age.

"I'd rather throw my ice cream at him than wave," Maggie replied.

"If you do, that will be the last ice cream I ever buy for you."

Maggie went silent then, and Christine changed the subject.

"Mom said I can finally give you that orange sweater you love, Abigail. I told Mom that I really don't want to stand out with any bright colors and, surprisingly enough, she conceded—with that sweater at least."

At the mention of leaving, all three kids drew closer to Christine's side and fought for one of her hands.

"I don't want to talk about you leaving," Abigail whispered.

Christine tried to lighten the mood by reminding them about the matching outfits Teresa used to buy them. "Hey, maybe Mom will buy us matching sailor suits again now that we are older. Remember the whistles in the pockets attached by lanyards? Putt Putt would probably want one, too."

"I think I will stick with your sweater," Abigail replied with a smile.

The orange sweater had been set aside during one of Teresa's strategic packing sessions. Christine had tried to put aside all the anxiety she felt when it came to clothes. Her mother had flourished with the responsibility of planning her school wardrobe, and they had made two shopping trips to the city that summer. Teresa's sister, Christine's Aunt Virginia, had even sent a taupe kilt skirt from Sak's Fifth Avenue to Christine as a gift. She included a note declaring it perfect for a Catholic school. It looked too short to Christine, but she didn't dare say a word.

Teresa was thrilled when it arrived, and she said, "Did you know that when I was just a little thing, Aunt Virginia bought me my first store-bought dress with her very first paycheck? She was ten years older than I, the oldest in our family, and she had gotten a job at the local candy store. I guess she felt sorry for me."

Christine was feeling sorry for herself with the abundance of new, fashionable clothes. But Teresa insisted that she would be living closer to the city and living alongside girls from privileged households. Simple and plain would have suited Christine better, but Teresa never asked her opinion on the clothing choices. It all felt so wasteful to her. She would rather wear hand-me-downs. Once, Francis's fiancée gave her some of her old clothes. Christine adored Francis's fiancée, Carol. So having her clothes felt very special. She also liked the feeling of having no choices when it came to clothes. These were the clothes God had given her, so they were simply perfect. All of the fun of the hand-me-downs had ended when she walked out into the living room in Carol's old sweater and jeans.

"Where did those come from?" Teresa had demanded. She disapproved of Christine's love of blue jeans and would sometimes sing a song about it to tease her.

Christine replied, crestfallen. "These were from Carol. Aren't they nice?"

"Why don't you donate them to the church. They need hand-me-downs more than we do."

Christine didn't feel that charity was her mother's first intention. She could hear the pride in her voice. On the trip down to school, she found herself daydreaming about weekend thrift-store shopping trips with the friends she was sure she would make. Her mother would never know.

"Picking out those school outfits for you reminded me of when my parents allowed me to pick out dresses from a Montgomery Ward catalog." Teresa flashed her gorgeous grin at Christine, breaking her from her daydream about thrifting. "Have I told you that story?"

"I don't think so. Will you tell it?" Christine was hoping something would calm the butterflies in her stomach.

"Well, I guess it can all point back to Old Gus, the hunchback who worked for us. He was a true hunchback. When he was younger, he had fallen through a hole into a basement and then lay in bed for ages, not healing correctly. So he was a real hunchback, and my parents kept him on the farm as help. If I close my eyes, I can still see his form, lumbering along among the shadows in the barnyard. Even with Gus on the farm, there were plenty of other jobs to go around to us kids. At that time, my parents asked me to take charge of a bummer lamb because they knew I always took my responsibilities very seriously.

As soon as I got off the school bus, I would get an old beer bottle and fill it with warm milk for my lamb. I never named him properly—I just called him 'baaa.' He would wait for me at the bus stop and then follow noisily at my heels as I went to get his bottle. Well, one day he wasn't there at the bus stop. My parents had gone to town, and I went all over searching for him. Finally, I went into the barn and there was Baaa's head, just lying on the ground."

"Oh no, Mom!" Christine cried out in horror.

Teresa lowered her voice for effect and said, "My parents had told Gus to butcher him and to get rid of all the evidence, you see. Gus had forgotten to get rid of the head. I didn't eat lamb again until I was 25. The upshot of it was that

I was so forlorn that my parents finally said I could order dresses from the Montgomery Ward catalog. I guess you could call it blood money, and I hated those dresses.

"That explains a lot," Christine replied. "Were the catalogs where you got your appreciation for fashion?"

"That is a good question," Teresa responded. "It could have been that, or maybe it was the fact that my family went through periods of being wealthy and periods of being very poor. One of the poor seasons was when I was in high school and we lived on a farm out in the country—I envied the wealthy town kids. We only had 25 cents each that year to buy Christmas gifts for each other."

"Was that due to the Depression?" Christine inquired.

"Actually, no. My father had lost everything before the Depression. He was a bootlegger, remember?"

"Oh yes! Please tell that story again. It is one of my favorites."

"Well, my father, Joseph, came from Kentucky, and I guess he couldn't shake those Kentucky ways. He must have had the recipe for Rye Whiskey etched permanently in his brain. When my parents first moved West, Father had worked as a grave digger. But with so many children coming along, he landed a job at the courthouse as a probation officer."

"Could you remind me of all the children's names?"

"Yes, first it was Carl, then Virginia, and Marion, then Joseph, or J.B., Dorothy—she always hated me. I don't know why. Maybe because I was closest in age. She was jealous, I guess. After me was Paul and then Anita."

"And J.B. was the one who died?"

"Yes, that was after the bootlegging. It's like my father's sins found him out. You see, we were relatively prosperous in those years when he was with the courthouse. We had a ranch outside of Sheridan, Wyoming, on the shores of Little Goose Creek. I loved it there. In the winter, we could strap on our skates and skate right from the house onto the frozen creek. But I guess my father wanted more, and he couldn't stay away from trouble. He started making rye whiskey up in the mountains outside of Sheridan—way out in the boonies—and he used his jailbirds to help him.

Before long, he got the sheriff involved, Frank Toy. My mother was so unhappy. As they grew richer, Father expected her to dress up and be more social. Soon, we had a home in town, not far from the courthouse. It had ten rooms. I'll never forget that gorgeous house. This was during Prohibition, you see. Alcohol was illegal. Sometimes, Father would take us out to the stills. I was very young, so I didn't really know what was going on at the time. It wouldn't be until years later that I recognized that sour smell of rye mash. Oh, it smelled awful! I just remember bouncing around on all the rocks as we drove out to the stills, and then I remember that awful smell.

Then the revenuers must have caught up with my father. My mother kept the clipping from the first page of the Casper Herald. It was 1924. Mother tried to hide it, but I was very snoopy. The article was titled, 'Two Sheridan Officers Quit.' It said that Charles Toy, Frank's brother, who had already resigned and was the undersheriff, and my father, Joseph, the janitor at the courthouse, had resigned due to their illegal activities. 'Bootleg scandals,' it said. I wonder if my father had been a janitor all along, not a probation officer? All the money must have come from the bootlegging. The article said that Charles Toy planned to go into the hotel business in Denver.

Then there was our family. Not all of us were home at the time since Virginia would often go stay with relatives in Billings for work. Marion had gotten a full scholarship to a school back east, so she wasn't home for the big scandal. The rest of us had to pack a few belongings in our red Dodge and leave during the night. It was awful for me. I loved school and I loved the nuns, and just like that, we were driving away from the ranch and the big house in town, and we were gone. We drove through the night to my uncle's farm in Idaho. I remember that first night, Dad had us sleep in the barn so that we wouldn't wake my uncle's family."

Christine remembered the barn and J. B.'s death now. It was all tied together. Her grandfather's wayward ways and the death of her uncle. She knew that the Bible said that the consequences of the sins of fathers and grandfathers would visit the children and the grandchildren. She felt cold all of a sudden and filled with dread. What if something happened to her family while she was away at school? Like what happened to J. B. when Aunt Marion was away.

As much as Christine liked to listen, it wasn't the same for talking. She would usually keep her thoughts and feelings to herself and then write them down later in her diary.

Her mother wasn't able to finish the story this time, as the time had passed quickly and they had reached the city of Pine Valley, where Mt. St. Paul's was located.

"We are here, Christine! Isn't it lovely? I have heard so much about it, but it is even more beautiful than I had imagined."

"Who told you about the school again, Mom?"

Teresa didn't seem to hear Christine as she craned her neck to look at the lovely St. Clement's church across the street from the school.

"Oh, I just wish I could move in with you, Chrissy. What a lovely haven this is, don't you agree?"

Christine did agree. Compared to the high desert of home, the abundant greenery and towering evergreens felt lush, and it smelled like Christmas. Christine looked at her mother then. Her eyes sparkled as if it were Christmas, her favorite time of year. She still wondered what motivated her mother. She was so full of life. Rather than excitement at the surroundings, Christine just felt sudden inner peace and calm. She felt like she had come home. The sooner she could get settled into her situation, the better. More than anything, she was looking forward to meeting the nuns. She would ask them about the sins of the fathers and the death of her young uncle. She would ask them to pray for her family while she was away.

Chapter 7

Edward was surprised to see Bishop James drive up just as they were pulling the wet carpets out. Alice must have told the bishop about Edward's disappearance when she reported the leak. The bishop parked his blue Buick in the alley and made his way to the church office. The parish secretary, Bonnie, murmured under her breath before making sure Edward was aware of the visit.

"What did you do now, Father? Take a hammer to the pipes? I'll cover for you if you want to get lost."

If Alice were puritanical, then Bonnie would be considered liberated. The two only pretended to get along.

Nearly two decades older than Alice, Bonnie did not give any weight to Alice's growing suspicions about Edward.

Bonnie murmured, "How is anyone supposed to win souls while we are hosting tea parties with the bishop?"

Edward gave Bonnie a pat on her shoulder and said, "Would you so kindly put the kettle on?"

"Anything for you, Father," Bonnie replied.

Bonnie had been with the parish long before Edward. In comparison, Alice was a newcomer. The rectory housekeeper, before Alice, had only lasted a year and a half when she blamed her exit on weak nerves. It was too much hosting a steady stream of parish wives who came over with the pretense of delivering fruit crisps and preserves, but who really only wanted a glimpse of Edward's private life.

Alice had simply put her foot down and told the women to take their baked goods to the rescue mission. "Father Edward doesn't indulge in sweets," she would tell them. Bonnie kept a stash of dark chocolates for Edward in her desk. It didn't take long for the housekeepers to realize that Bonnie was Edward's favorite.

Bonnie's husband, Joe, had been gone before Edward's time, but from Bonnie's constant remembrance, Edward felt Joe would have been one of his closest friends.

"If Joe were here, he would send the bishop packing! What does the bishop know about running this church with a face like yours? I don't mean any ill will, but the bishop's face is one that only a mother could love. You, on the other hand, Father Edward, are what Joe would call a real dreamboat. What was your mother thinking, sending you off to be a priest? You would have thought she would be dreaming of all the beautiful grandbabies you could give her."

Edward would just smile and appreciate that Bonnie didn't require responses from him. She understood him. He pointed toward the door just as the bishop approached it.

Bonnie turned on her charm, "Good morning, Bishop James! The tea will be ready in a jiffy. To what do we owe this honor?"

The bishop ignored her question but gave her a kind smile and told her he would take his tea in Edward's office.

"Shall we?" The bishop gestured for Edward to go in, and then he shut the door.

"Bonnie sure has a lot of vim and vigor—nothing slows her down. Are you sure she is good for you, Edward?"

Edward knew better than to show any favoritism. It was a game that he was stuck in. Show indifference to the people he liked and favoritism to the ones he didn't.

The bishop continued. "Thankfully, we have Alice watching over things here. Don't you agree?"

"She is the best," Edward nodded. "A real keeper."

"I'm concerned for you, Edward. Alice said you have been unaccounted for on numerous occasions, including this morning. What were you thinking, disappearing while there was a real emergency?"

Edward gave him a smile and replied, "It's good for Earl to feel needed. His kids said as much." It didn't take much to get the kindly Bishop James off his tail.

"I did hear that, yes. His family has been good to us. You would never know that he was slipping when he gets his tools in his hands. Alice said he had everything as right as rain faster than a minnow can swim a dipper. It's too bad about the carpets, but the insurance will cover that. Do you want to help pick out the new ones?"

"Sure, that would be fine," Edward replied. Bonnie would handle it for him.

Edward knew that the bishop's heart was in the right place and that he carried a significant burden overseeing the many rural churches that made up the Diocese of Delta City. It was no secret that problem priests were sent to the most rural of churches. But after Edward planted a church in a small town up north, the diocese was happy to send him to plant a larger church in Delta City and then to serve as the parish priest in Pine Valley. In reality, the diocese knew Edward could get the numbers up. St. Clement's was full every service. Edward hoped it was his sermons and people's desire for the Lord in their lives, not he himself, that kept people coming. Either way, the bishop's visits didn't worry him. It was all part of the process.

"How are your ulcers faring, Your Excellency? I do hope you have found some relief?"

The bishop sat forward in his chair and put his chin in his hand. "I'm not sure anything is working too well. Maybe all the Jello is helping. It is hard because everyone offers me coffee and beer. I am thankful for you and Bonnie having this, what is it, marshmallow tea? It means a lot. You know I like coming here to see you. Really, Edward, how are you doing?"

Edward sat in silence a moment before saying, "One need not cry out very loudly; He is nearer to us than we think."

"Don't get philosophical on me again, Edward. That isn't really answering my question."

Edward had been memorizing Brother Lawrence's words, and it was throwing the bishop off course.

Edward just smiled and changed the subject. "What other areas have you been visiting lately?"

"Don't even get me started," Bishop James sighed. "You know how long a drive it is to Alturas, and they have been sending me there weekly. Please don't mention it, but I just don't get on well with Father Sullivan. Maybe what they say about him is true, and this doesn't help my ulcers at all. I spend six hours fretting on the way there, get an icy reception when I arrive, and then have to stay overnight. The six-hour drive back home seals the deal. I feel it takes me two days to recover. Then I have to write the reports, and the whole ordeal may as well take up my whole week. I look forward to getting called up here to see you, and then my Alturas visits get postponed. Father Sullivan has talked about returning to Ireland. Would you add that possibility to your prayers?"

Edward steadied his gaze on the bishop and said, "Why don't we just pray right now?"

Bishop James leaned forward and said, "Maybe your philosophy isn't so bad. I like that about you—you cut through all the rules and preconceptions and just get down to business."

Edward began praying for the people of Alturas under Father Sullivan's influence, that he might return to Ireland and relieve the bishop of his burden. He prayed for Bishop James's ulcers and then mentioned his own flock at St. Clement's. He simply ended his prayer with "It's in your name, Jesus, that we pray."

Bishop James gave him a look and asked where he learned to pray like that.

Edward pushed his glasses back up into place and replied, "The gospel of John simply says we can ask for things in the name of the Son."

"So true, so true," the bishop responded before changing the subject. "How are your teams doing? I still don't understand your allegiance to the Chicago Cubs. I would love to hear the whole story this time."

Edward knew the bishop liked just sitting and listening, so he drew a deep breath and resolved to give him that opportunity. "I am not sure you would approve, but I joined allegiance with the Cubs after meeting a protestant preacher, Billy Sunday, back home at Mary Lake. It must have been a streak of rebellion to pick a team other than my family's favorite, the Cincinnati Reds.

One weekend, my father had also displayed a rebellious streak. Rather than head to Emerald City with my mother's family, my father had declared he would be taking me to Mary Lake for the weekend instead. Some boys might have been excited at the prospect of a father-son weekend, but that hadn't been the case for me.

My father was a stern and quiet man—I don't think I had ever seen him smile. Like my mother, he had come from German stock, but unlike her, they were poor. The money was all from my mother's side of the family. My father worked hard as a plumber, but he must have always felt the weight of marrying up. I think our father-son weekend was more about putting his foot down, rather than making it enjoyable for me.

I can still see the look of disapproval on my mother's face as she posed a question that sounded more like a statement, 'You will be back for Sunday services?'

To which my father replied, 'We should be, but don't be concerned if we get held up.'

You see, my brother had drowned on a Sunday morning waiting for my father to show up."

Bishop James nodded solemnly. He enjoyed these times when Edward would open up about his past—there was almost nothing he enjoyed more, in fact.

Edward continued, "We left Franklin early for Mary Lake so that we could get in a full day of fishing. The image of my father, staring ahead at the lake, holding his fishing pole, is etched into my memory. He truly was like a statue in my life—there was never any animation. He was very handsome, and I'm sure he had been quite a catch for my mother. He was welcomed into her notorious family, with all their money, and didn't need to contribute much. He was like an accessory to the family—the trajectory of his life had been set out before him, and he just needed to step into the picture. The death of my brother was not supposed to be part of the story, and that must have been when he first considered stepping out of that picture."

"That would make sense," the bishop offered. "Please continue."

"Well, my father offered no help with my fishing line—beyond the first cast. I heard a lively conversation down a ways from where we were fishing. I slowly drifted toward the spot where the two men were visiting.

'You do know that I used to play for the Cubs, or as I still like to call them, the White Stockings?' This man looked to be as old as my grandfather, but with a very athletic build. My grandfather had been quite portly.

'Everyone knows that, Sunday.' The younger gentleman replied. 'But you also played for the Phillies? Why do you still like the Cubs?'

I couldn't believe I was overhearing an actual baseball player, and soon I was standing right by his side.

The man saw me and smiled, but kept up with his conversation, "I am loyal to the Cubs because Chicago is loyal to me. Some of my most rewarding work is in Chicago with the Pacific Garden Mission. Indeed, the very same place where I met my Lord.'

I was enthralled with the man's speech and the casual way he mentioned the Lord.

The other man said, 'Yes, we all know that you were a professional baseball player turned evangelist.'

I surprised myself by saying then, 'Sir, what is an evangelist?'

The baseball player turned to me and flashed a mischievous grin my way, 'Well, Son, just going to church doesn't make you a Christian any more than going to a garage makes you an automobile, and, if you are a stranger to prayer, you are a stranger to the greatest source of power known to mortals. An evangelist helps people get acquainted with Jesus, who is the light of the world and who hears every prayer. My name is Billy Sunday, and whom do I have the pleasure of speaking with?'

I shook his hand then and said, 'My name is Edward.'

'It is nice to meet you, Edward. Do you go to church?'"

Just then, Alice opened the door, and the men heard Bonnie exclaim, "I am so sorry, Reverends. Alice insisted on just barging in."

"That is what I was hired for, Bonnie. To keep Father Edward on track, his calendar is completely booked today."

Bishop James stood up and said, "All good things must come to an end, it seems. May we continue this conversation another day, Father Edward? I am really curious as to what else this Sunday character said."

"It would be my pleasure, Your Excellency. I will think about that conversation and try to remember more of what he said. I believe he had quite an influence on me, and his sudden death, while I was still in seminary, was a big loss."

"Who is a 'Sunday character,' I would like to know?" Alice said.

Bonnie replied under her breath, "I believe the reverends know more 'Sunday characters' than we could count. Leave them alone, Alice—their business is not yours."

Bishop James laughed at Bonnie's joke and then lifted his hands in a calming gesture, "Now, now, ladies, it is alright. We were speaking of a man named Billy Sunday. Now that Father Edward mentions it, I have heard of him before—in my work with the homeless. He was very outspoken concerning drunkenness and the way it contributed to homelessness. I believe Sunday once said that 'Jesus Christ was God's revenue officer.'"

As the women grumbled in response, Edward took those words to heart and hoped he would have time alone to ponder them further—along with his memories from the shores of Mary Lake.

Chapter 8

As she and her mother made their way through the front doors of Mt. St. Paul's, Christine tried to empty her mind of things like her grandpa getting caught by revenuers, a hunchback with an ax, and her mother's lamb's head lying on the barn floor.

This was a new start for Christine. Just as soon as she could, she would go to a thrift store to buy some plain clothes and be rid of all the costumes her mother had packed. On the trip down, Christine had decided she was more excited to meet the nuns than the girls her age. She had a sudden craving to be away from all the world's cares.

A layperson, Mrs. Horne, welcomed them and started them on a tour of the school. She saw her mother's look of disapproval as she assessed Mrs. Horne. Christine knew exactly what her mother was thinking—she no doubt disapproved of Mrs. Horne's dated hairstyle and clothing, but especially of the extra five pounds around her waist. Teresa never shied away from giving her opinion on people's appearances—like the comment Christine couldn't shake, the one when her mother told her that one side of her face was prettier than the other.

"Chrissy, you should always part your hair to the right and wear bangs. Your left side is the good side of your face, and bangs help you look less severe. And, while you are at school, don't forget to put the Scotch tape on your forehead at night to stop those furrows from getting deeper between your eyes."

Please God, help me, Christine said to herself. Just listen to Mrs. Horne, she told herself.

"This will be your homeroom, Christine. Wait, do you go by Christine or Chrissy?"

She and her mother answered at the same time.

Teresa said, "She goes by Chrissy."

Christine said, "I go by Christine."

Her mother slowly turned her head around and gave her an odd look.

"Sorry," Mrs. Horne said. "Which one is it?"

With a shaky voice, Christine repeated, "I go by Christine now."

"That is so pretty," Mrs. Horne replied. "Were you named after St. Christina?"

Teresa cleared her throat in annoyance and answered, "No, she wasn't named after a saint, that's for sure."

Christine didn't know what to think. All of her siblings had been named after saints, so she always figured that she had as well. Why was her mother acting like that?

Mrs. Horne distracted her by saying, "Well, this will be your homeroom, Christine, so this is where you will come first thing tomorrow morning at 8:00. Breakfast is at 7:30, and you have the option of chapel at 6 with the nuns. The girls rarely go, but don't forget that you have the option."

Christine had been hoping for a chance to worship with the nuns.

Mrs. Horne walked along at a fast pace and pointed out the girls' bathroom next.

"As you know by now, boys only come for classes during the day. There are no boy boarders. This is one of the girls' bathrooms. There are more options upstairs by the dormitory."

Christine was thankful there were more options. She had been shy about using public bathrooms for as long as she could remember, since that incident with her stepfather.

One of her first memories of Patrick—her mother had married him when she was three—was of her using the bathroom nearest the living room in their new house, where he was reading the newspaper. She was still so pleased to be potty trained and took her time going through all the steps. Her childhood up until that point, essentially living homeless in the forest, had been so wild and free, including her bathroom habits.

Christine was talking to herself as she went through all the steps she had recently been taught. She had just finished drying her hands and was refolding the hand towel when she heard Patrick say to her mother, "I'd better never have to hear her bathroom noises again. Tell her to run the water when she uses the toilet."

Christine had felt ashamed in the bathroom ever since. That incident—her first distinct memory of Patrick—felt like the end of her carefree childhood. But this was a new beginning now—a new freedom—at Mt. St. Paul's. She was already far from Patrick and ready to embrace what was dear to her.

Mrs. Horne was leading them up the stairs when a nun, who was walking down the stairs, met them at a landing. "Oh, this is Sister Mary Rita, Christine," Mrs. Horne exclaimed. "Sister Mary Rita, please meet Christine, an incoming freshman, and her mother, Mrs. Harrison."

"It is very nice to meet you, Christine, and you, Mrs. Harrison. I trust you are settling in well?"

Christine started to answer, but Teresa spoke up first, "I was so excited for this day when Christine would become acquainted with nuns!" Christine shrank back in the corner as her mother continued.

"I attended Catholic schools for most of my childhood. I was close to the nuns, especially in grammar school. I remember one time jumping rope while the nuns watched. We had to wait a long time for our turn to jump and, when it was my turn, I tried my hardest to keep my place." Teresa laughed. "One day, I was jumping so fast, with great exuberance, that my bloomers fell down around my ankles. The nuns had their hands to their mouths to cover their laughter."

"I imagine you brought them much delight," Sister Mary Rita responded kindly. "Was that in California?"

"Oh, no," Teresa replied. "That was in Wyoming before we moved to Idaho. In Idaho, I attended St. Joe's. We were called Cat-Lickers by all the Mormons there. I haven't liked them since."

Christine didn't think Sister Mary Rita knew what to say then, but her habit raised a bit with her eyebrows.

Mrs. Horne saved the day then by saying, "We must not keep you, Reverend Mother. I will take Christine and Mrs. Harrison to the dormitory now."

"Good day, Christine and Mrs. Harrison. I will look forward to more time with you soon, Christine." Sister Mary Rita gave Christine a warm smile before nodding to Teresa.

Christine relished the sound of the nun's skirts swishing as she continued down the stairs.

They walked down a long corridor and came to a large room at the end with rows of beds and dressers between each bed.

"And here is the dormitory," Mrs. Horne said, extending her hand with a flourish. "You may choose whichever one you like. The Bible you see on the pillow is our gift to you, and the beds that haven't been taken will still have the Bibles there."

Christine could not hide her excitement then. Imagine, her very own Bible. Her mother had given her a prayer book, but she had never owned a Bible. She nearly ran forward to inspect the beds that had not been taken. She was surprised to see that the one nearest the window hadn't been chosen yet. She rushed to the window and saw that it overlooked the chapel, surrounded on one side by evergreen trees.

As if reading her thoughts, Mrs. Horne said, "Those are incense cedars. Aren't they magnificent?"

"Oh, yes," Christine responded. "I don't believe we have those around Alturas."

"Of course we do," Teresa jumped in. "Why do you think they call the pass Cedar Pass?" For Mrs. Horne's benefit, she added, "We have a small ski hill not far from our house, and there are some pockets where the incense cedar grows. But I don't think Chrissy enjoys skiing quite as much as her older brothers and me. It hasn't been that long since I attempted a ski jump with the boys and broke my leg in several places, requiring surgery. It is a good thing we have our hired help, Cordelia."

Christine felt shy and small again but was able to say, almost in a whisper, "I'd like to take this bed, Mrs. Horne."

Mrs. Horne gave Christine's shoulders a squeeze and said, "I think it was nothing short of providential."

Teresa ran a hand over the dresser and asked, "There must be a closet somewhere? It won't be suitable for Christine to cram her clothes in these small drawers."

Christine felt mortified and started to say that it would be all right.

Mrs. Horne winked at her and answered, "There is no cause for concern. I think we can make some arrangements for Christine. Remember that each dresser has to be rented. Would you like two for Christine, as well as extra closet space?"

Teresa nodded, "I guess that will have to do."

Christine didn't want any special arrangements. In fact, she had just recently read parts of Anthony's college psychology book. It indicated that giving a child too much attention can lead to shyness. It is as if the child is made to believe that the world revolves around them. She read that this can cause anxiety when the child thinks it is up to them to make everyone happy. They also believe that everyone is thinking about them, and they don't want to disappoint them—thus the shyness.

That first night, as she lay in her bed by the window, all the Fritos she had eaten on the trip south, or perhaps nervousness, seemed to catch up with Christine, and she ran to the bathroom to be sick. She heard a knock outside the stall, then Sister Mary Rita's soft voice, "Are you ok, Dear?"

It's ok, Christine told herself, this is normal. Patrick isn't here, and it is ok to be normal.

"Yes," Christine answered. "I will be right out."

Sister Mary Rita was waiting for Christine outside the bathroom and then helped clean her face with a cool cloth.

After she walked Christine to her bed, she said, "I will be praying for you tonight."

Back in her bed, Christine realized this was her first night away from her family. Her mother didn't allow overnights with friends until they were in high school. Christine knew there were things she would miss from home—like offering a listening ear to her siblings, her mother, and her friends—but she was also ready to spend more time listening to God.

There would be no more late nights with the din of her mother's fights with Patrick. There would be the nuns' rules and order, and the nuns keeping a prayerful watch over them.

I will be prayed for, Christine thought. Have I ever been prayed for?

"Pray for me, please," Christine whispered, without a thought to whom she might be pleading.

The Liturgy of Father Edward

Chapter 9

Edward risked serious repercussions with the diocese when he began turning down his parishioners' weekly dinner invitations. But all the idle talk and self-indulgence were making him ill, and he saw this repulsion as a good thing—something good for his soul.

He lost his appetite for wine overnight. At first, he faked it by just drinking a little at the Pedigraws. But the last time he refused the wine altogether, followed by refusing the dinner invitation for the following week.

Mrs. Pedigraw had been speechless and the next morning had tried phoning Alice, not Bonnie, before finally calling Bishop James herself.

"Something has gotten into him, Bishop. That is all I can say. You'd better keep a close eye on him."

With a more open schedule, Edward was finding time to visit Dochero as often as three times a week. He left before dawn and, at first, would smoke his morning cigarette once he had arrived. He had found a spot beneath the bridge, far off the trail. After lighting his cigarette, like a warm companion, he would think and pray—one of his prayers being that his time there would not coincide with Margaret's.

Dochero brought out something in him that was hard to pinpoint. The mornings unfolded the same way every time. He woke in the dark, feeling lonely. It was as if God were hiding Himself in those early, dark hours. Desperate thoughts came easily to Edward during that time, and the only way to shake them was to set out on a search. A new day and a new search for God.

Waking each morning before sunrise, closer to 4:30, Edward would quietly leave the house and then pause a moment to make sure Margaret's house was still quiet as well. From there, he would walk briskly, avoiding street lamps and porch lights. With his mind groggy and slow, Edward could only find the words that came easily to him, and he repeated them over and over as he walked, "Lord have mercy, Lord have mercy." He was searching and waiting for God to reveal Himself.

"We have to start afresh every day," Edward mumbled as he arrived at the bridge and at Dochero.

These stolen moments at Dochero were the first time in Edward's adult life that he allowed himself to be flooded by memories. Or maybe it was the first time he had given those memories his undivided attention—especially the painful ones.

His departure for seminary seemed to coincide with his parents' midlife crises. Edward was a big believer in the midlife crisis. He believed it was something God used to define each person in the second half of their life. It was as if the midlife crisis were a significant juncture at which an individual could press into the Lord or walk away from Him. Will they be a kind, peaceful, and humble person for the rest of their days, or self-focused and prideful—hiding within thick walls of shame? If a person chose the latter, it was a slippery slope for their lost soul.

These crises started in many forms, and as a priest, Edward had seen them all. The classic crises included marital affairs and plastic surgeries, gym memberships, and one too many cats. Evidence of hoarding became hard to hide for some, and for others, they became obsessed with politics and the cares of home ownership.

"I need to find another landscaper—no one seems to know how to properly edge a lawn these days," a male parishioner would say.

At the exact moment, his wife might be talking to a friend, "Do you think pale yellow wallpaper is a sensible choice? I am thinking of redoing the living room as a cure for my empty nesting blues."

The husband would continue his bemoaning that there were no good workers to be found, and he sure wished his "deadbeat son would come around and offer to help once in a while."

These obsessions would take over the person's whole life and very being. If they didn't snap out of it soon, it literally snowballed until they entered eternity.

Was this Edward's midlife crisis? The dark night of his soul? Preferring a child's make-believe spot, Dochero, to the company of his parishioners?

Edward knew he was soothing himself with memories from home, but he decided to let it happen and see what came out of it.

His parents' midlife crises had reached a head by the time he left for seminary. Edward liked to believe that his father's weekend trips to Mary Lake were innocent—and they probably were. Just a man, his thoughts, and a fishing pole. Edward never learned that anything more had come out of them. But that didn't stop Edward's mother from accusing her husband of sordid things. Edward thought the grief of losing George had caught up with both of them, and they had started to lead separate lives.

It was a relief to Edward, then, to have his sights set on seminary. They had raised him for this moment after all. The only wrench that Edward threw in was that he wanted to attend St. Joseph's seminary in Chicago, not St. Joseph's in Ohio.

"I don't understand, Edward. How did you even hear of St. Joseph's in Chicago? All of your uncles went to St. Joe's—it is a family tradition, and the fees are much reduced." His mother had pleaded with him.

Edward lied, "I heard some kids talking about it. The seminary in Chicago has a solid reputation for putting out good priests. I want to go west when I am ordained, like a missionary. I might as well start making my way over now."

It was like his mother's heart was breaking all over again, but Edward was stubborn. He didn't want to tell them that Billy Sunday had recommended St. Joseph's in Chicago that day by the shores of Mary Lake. Edward had explained to Sunday about his family's wealthy, Catholic heritage. Billy Sunday had actually already been familiar with some of Edward's grandfather's church architecture.

"Didn't your grandfather also build the YMCA in Franklin?"

Edward had replied that he had lost count of how many buildings his grandfather had built.

Sunday had continued to explain that he had given up his baseball career to share Jesus with the broken and the outcasts at the Chicago YMCA. He had heard of the work being done at the YMCA in Franklin.

This was mind-blowing for young Edward to hear that a baseball star had given up his career to become an evangelist.

Baseball was an obsession in Edward's family. The men in his family, including the religious, had always sat out on the front porch with the radio and a bottle of whiskey to listen to the games. Gigi wouldn't believe it when he told her that he had met a famous baseball player who didn't even drink alcohol.

Sunday had gone silent for a while when Edward told him that he was going to become a priest. He finally spoke out, "Many of my protestant friends heavily criticize Catholics, but I will not say a word against them. I have seen very dedicated Catholic priests among the missionaries at Pacific Garden Mission. They humbly serve the homeless without demanding recognition, some even sleep nights out on the streets—like a Fool for Christ."

"A Fool for Christ?" Edward thought to himself. He had never heard that phrase.

Sunday continued, "Son, if you become a Catholic priest, I pray you will put servitude to Christ above all and that you will leave behind the indulgences and temptations of the world. That you will become poor on earth so that you will be rich in eternity. That you will be a Fool for Christ. As soon as you become a priest, it will be like you have a target on your back. A target for the devil's ways and also a target for people who will want to distract you from your calling. Why don't you see about coming to Chicago for seminary? Maybe then you can spend time at Pacific Garden Mission. I will see you there if you do."

That weekend at Mary Lake had been life-changing for Edward. He threatened his parents that he would run away and forsake the priesthood if he could not go to St. Joseph's in Chicago. It was tough to see his mother's tears, but then again, they were commonplace in their home.

Edward could not believe all that had transpired since meeting Sunday at Mary Lake, and then later at the mission in Chicago. Why hadn't he remembered Sunday's words until now?

Edward had been indulgent. He had also been lazy—too comfortable among the riches of his parishioners. "Way too comfortable," he thought, cringing at the memory.

Gradually, during those mornings at Dochero, Edward had also stopped finishing his one cigarette.

"Your fingers are about to get burned." A voice pounced on him from out of the trees one morning.

Edward jumped, and the cigarette's lengthening ember fell onto his hand.

"Why must you startle me? How long have you been there?" Edward asked Margaret as he plunged his hand into the creek, nearly losing his new glasses in the process.

"Long enough to see that you don't care much for those cigarettes anymore."

"That is something, isn't it? I think you are right."

"How did you manage to shake the habit? My parents can never quit anything for more than three days. Maybe it is the magic of this place."

"I don't believe in magic, and neither should you. But what do you mean, 'this place?'"

"Well, my father thinks it is magic because someone found a big gold nugget in the creek several years ago, a five-pound one! So my father thinks there could be miracles in the water. Maybe that is why you don't want to smoke anymore."

"It's hard to say. The change sort of snuck up on me. I don't seem to care much about anything anymore. Everything in the world seems to be losing its shine."

"You sound depressed to me," Margaret said. "But I have good news—I know a cure. My mom's fried chicken. I told my mom that I see you here from time to time, at your 'Dochero.' Once she got over the shock and asked twenty questions—she almost called the police on you, you know. Well then, she decided that it might be fun to cook her famous fried chicken for you and have you to dinner. What do you say?"

Lately, Edward had been telling the parishioners no so often that he surprised himself by quickly saying, "Well, yes. That does sound good. That is very nice of your mother. I am supposed to consult my housekeeper and the church receptionist, but I do think my calendar is quite clear. Shall we say Wednesday?"

"Wednesdays are good, I think. Unless there is a baseball game on, and then my dad will be three sheets to the wind."

"I think we can manage either way, but I believe that Wednesday is pretty safe where baseball is concerned."

And that was the pattern the Dochero mornings took for Edward. Each morning unfolded like one of God's mysteries. It was pretty simple in his mind—God hides Himself, Edward searches for Him, God reveals Himself. It was up to Edward to keep searching.

Chapter 10

"Christine. Christine. Wake up, Dear," Sister Mary Rita whispered. It was 5:45 a.m. and the bells were ringing for chapel. Christine was one of only two girls at Mt. St. Paul's who had expressed a desire to attend Vigils with the nuns. Some girls made fun of her and Nancy for it, while some admired them, but not enough to forego the extra hour of sleep each morning.

Due to tiredness and a wandering mind, Christine admittedly failed to hear about half of the morning's psalms and prayers—but it was as if she became addicted to the ritual. It felt special to wake to the bells, and Sister Mary Rita's whispers, and to dress in the chill and the dark. The sound of the nuns' habits as they rushed up the stairs brought a feeling of urgency—of importance. Christine and Nancy, with the nuns, were sanctifying the day for the Lord's use.

My heart is ready, O God, my heart is ready.

The lack of sacredness back at home had always bothered Christine.

Truth be told, Teresa had a very naughty streak she had inherited from her father and, rather than put it to death, seemed to nurture it. Teresa regularly sang songs around the house, like "Caviar comes from virgin sturgeon."

"No, Mom, please!" Christine would plead.

"Why are you such a prude?" Teresa would reply. "Test the water a little. I'm not sure where you came from. Life is more fun with a little spunk, my dad would always say. It sure was lively in our house, like the time I gave my sisters a bowl of chicken manure and told them it was peanut butter. My dad was so proud of me!"

You would have thought that Teresa's father would have mended his ways after losing everything to the revenuers, and then with a chain of events culminating in the death of his son. It took many more hard years and indiscretions, however, to bring about change. Christine had heard that part of her mother's story more than once and more than she wanted to.

"My mother used to have us check the odometer on our father's car during the time that he was running around with a bad crowd. I felt like such a sneak! He was seeing another woman, so my mother was calculating his mileage. Another clue to his infidelity was the store-bought pastries he brought home to us at night. That woman must have worked at the bakery. My siblings and I loved all the extra sugar in those treats compared to the home-baked goods.

My mother, Theodora, was as saintly as her patron saint—she stood up to my father, a moment I will never forget.

We were all tucked into bed one night when we heard Mother say, 'Joe, if you leave tonight, don't ever bother coming back.' I held my breath during the silence that followed—wondering what would happen. First, there was a single thud, followed by a long silence. Then, there was a second thud. My father had let both of his shoes drop to the ground, one at a time. That was that—the running around stopped.

My father was smart as a whip and very hardworking, despite his faults. He kept our farm going, invested in the stock market, and also worked at the post office. He had landed back on his feet after bootlegging and even survived the Depression by selling out before the stock market crash—he advised others to do the same. He was a very sharp man, but couldn't pass up opportunities to misbehave. After he got caught stealing coal from the post office, and after Mother put an end to his philandering ways, it was then that he started paying us kids to pray for him." Teresa giggled, "That worked out well for us! This was about the same time I mailed in for some perfume samples to sell. I was supposed to mail most of the money back to the perfume seller, but I spent it on candy instead—along with my dad's prayer money."

Christine did not find any of this funny, though her brothers thought it was hilarious. Her older brothers were all known to get into their share of trouble.

"Paying for prayers?" Christine asked warily.

"I said the prayers, don't worry," Teresa responded. "But I did have a pretty guilty conscience by then, especially when the perfume people sent a letter to the house asking for the money. What did they expect? It was just vanilla anyway, not real perfume like my Estée Lauder. But, oh, were my parents ever upset with me! My dad made me help with his mail delivery to earn the money. He kept the money until he was ready to mail it. His mistake was giving it to me to mail for him. I took the money and spent it on candy. What did he expect? The apple didn't fall far from the tree. I was lucky that the perfume people never sent another letter. But I got to where I felt guilty even when I wasn't."

Christine didn't like the sounds of that. She didn't like feeling guilty even for a second. Listening to her mother made her think again about the sins of the fathers visiting the next generations.

Not just the sins of the fathers, Christine thought, "My sins, too."

Christine sometimes got dragged into her mom's schemes, and, in one incident in particular, she felt the need to confess over and over.

It had been a rare, tranquil night in their household of ten. Francis and Joseph were back at college after their Thanksgiving break, and Anthony was gone for his year at boarding school. Samuel was staying at a ranch to help with winter feeding, and Patrick had taken the younger kids to see his family over in the valley. He only took his biological children to see them. With all the twists and turns in Christine's life, she had managed to have almost no grandparent interactions. But there was rarely a lull in her bright and lively mother's activities.

That night in late November, Christine had just curled up by the fire with her notebook. She enjoyed writing poetry and was hoping to make some headway.

"Chrissy! We need a Christmas tree!" Teresa burst into the room and flashed her brilliant smile—Christine's quiet was over.

"Right now?" Christine asked. "It's already dark out."

"That's alright," Teresa responded. "Hurry and bundle up."

Christine felt the usual dread that came with her mother's ideas, but she obediently went to get her winter gear. She imagined hiking up the ski hill, in the snow, to cut down a tree. Her mother already had hot chocolate in a thermos, and the old Willys Jeep warmed up by the time Christine emerged.

"Are we headed to Cedar Pass?" she asked.

"Of course not, silly, I have a better idea," Teresa said, putting the jeep into gear.

Christine just sat, numbly, as her mom weaved through the frozen neighborhoods. What was she doing, planning to rob the Christmas tree lot? Every once in a while, Teresa slowed down and peered into the starlit yards.

Before long, they were in Diane's neighborhood, the girl Christine was hoping to befriend. Teresa came to a stop a short distance from her house. "Oh, look, they must have cut down an extra. Let's go try it out for our house."

Christine's feet felt like they were welded to the floorboard. She could see through the windows, and the family looked to be playing a board game. Diane's dad wasn't always at the bar like Teresa had suggested.

"Chrissy, come on, I need your help." Her mother's voice deepened.

"But, Mom, we can't. That's stealing."

Teresa laughed, "We aren't even sure we will want this one. Plus, they probably cut down two. You know how picky Diane's mother can be."

Christine never disobeyed her mother, so she opened the door with what felt like frozen fingers and stiffly walked over.

Her mother indicated for her to be quiet, then beckoned her over to the tree. They grabbed it and dragged it back through the snow to the Jeep. Her mother skillfully situated it on top and secured it with a rope she had brought along. All the way back to the house, she tried to get Christine to join her in singing Christmas carols.

"I'm not sure why you have to be such a spoil sport, Chrissy. Your brothers have always been game. What did you think that your stepfather was cutting the trees all these years? He only took us a time or two so that he could pose for all of those pictures."

Teresa was referring to those photographs where they looked like the picture-perfect family out in the snow with their freshly cut tree. In one picture, the older boys and Patrick were pulling the tree through the snow, with the younger children riding on top. Her family did these photo shoots periodically over the years. Sometimes Teresa would even insist on pictures of just Christine by herself or of Christine and her together.

"I guess I didn't put much thought into where the trees came from," Christine responded.

Once home, she hoped to get back to the fire and to her poetry, but then Teresa announced that the tree wasn't tall enough.

"Back on the hunt we go!" She exclaimed with excitement.

Christine wanted to die. Hunting was her mother's favorite hobby, not hers—especially when the hunting turned into poaching. This was a nightmare. She dutifully climbed back in the Jeep but felt frozen to the core.

This time, Teresa started singing "Christine the Christmas Tree", trying to get Christine into the mood. Teresa pulled back into her tracks near Diane's house. "See?" She said. "No harm done. And don't you just love this song? It is where I got your name after all."

Christine had heard that one before, but once her mom had also said she was named after Christ because she was her mother's miracle child. Christine didn't know what to think, and she had mixed feelings about the song and about her name.

After putting Diane's tree back at her house, Teresa dragged Christine along as they walked a few houses down and came to a stop in front of Jim Howard's house. Teresa didn't like Jim, a notorious man in town, due to a disagreement over his family's local sporting goods store. Teresa had tried to get a good deal on ammunition and was refused. Sure enough, there was a freshly cut tree leaning against Jim's fence.

"That one looks perfect, and I won't have a bit of guilt taking that scoundrel's tree. You know what they say, 'bad beginning, happy ending!'"

"Oh, Mom, really? What if we get caught?" Christine moaned.

"Come on, don't ruin the Christmas spirit. Sometimes I wonder where you came from. Remind me not to take you next time—spoilsport."

Christine went through all the motions of helping her mom, but she felt sick. Jim Howard's tree was perfect, and she mostly just sat and watched as her mom decorated it one-handed—a martini in the other hand. Teresa looked over at Christine sitting on the couch and said, "Attempting your poetry again? How about you write down something like this from James Metcalfe? It sounds just like you, and then maybe it will inspire your own writing—

"Kristina loves her blue jeans, and she wears them every day. Regardless of the weather or what anyone may say. In school, at play, to parties, and wherever you may search, except of course on Sunday when Kristina goes to church. She thinks no other article is quite so much in style, and when she puts those blue jeans on, she always wears a smile. She has a dozen dresses and perhaps a dozen more. But they just rest on hangars or they sleep upon the floor. The blue jeans are her favorite, as she has often said, and if she could, I know she would be wearing them to bed."

Teresa laughed and added, "It's true! No matter how many dresses I buy you, I can't seem to get you to like anything but those blue jeans! Maybe I should give them all to Phyllis? Perhaps she would be thankful."

The more Teresa sang and recited poems, the less Christine could focus on her own poetry. She was feeling torn. She couldn't think of anything she loved more than her home and her mother, but something wasn't right. This wasn't right. Stealing a Christmas tree? That is not the Christmas spirit.

Those torn feelings are what had pushed her into the arms of Mt. St. Paul's and into the rhythms of a prayerful life with the nuns. Christine was searching for something more pure, something untarnished. Did that exist in this world? Her teacher in homeroom was Sister Monica, and Christine clung to what she said one day—

"It is good when we experience the broken things of life, when we feel the brokenness deep inside, when we grieve the loss of perfection and, yet, still long for perfection. It is that longing for perfection that shows we are made for something better, and that there is something better. Don't ever give up on that longing for perfection. The trick is to realize that perfection will never be found in this life, only in Heaven. People who count on perfection in this life will soon tire, and they may give up altogether."

Christine did not want to give up. Not giving up meant she attended chapel whenever she could. Nothing had become more comforting than the sounds of the habits giving way to silence when they were all on their knees in the chapel. Blue jeans weren't allowed at Mt. St. Paul's, and Christine relished the idea of always wearing simple skirts like the nuns—she had found some at the local thrift store. "At least Mother would be happy to know that I have ditched the jeans," Christine thought as she knelt on her spot on the floor. Slowly, the silence was filled with those faithful, familiar words—sanctifying the day ahead and turning her thoughts to the holy.

Lord, our Savior, give us life!

Chapter 11

On Monday, Bishop James paid a visit to Edward in response to Mrs. Pedigraw's frantic calls. Bonnie lifted her eyebrows and then winked at Edward as she opened the door for Bishop James to enter his office.

"You do seem to be going through something, Edward," the bishop said with kindness and concern in his eyes. "However, how can I object to your sudden abstinence from cigarettes and alcohol. But I have to ask, how will you survive the rigors of the ministry now?"

With that, the bishop chuckled.

"It is strange," Edward agreed. "But I feel a new sense of purpose coming on and more peace inside than I remember experiencing before. I used to think I needed alcohol to survive the rigors of life, but now I am learning to lean on God, moment by moment, for the strength."

"Please tell me more," Bishop James asked.

Edward pushed his glasses back up, disappointed again that his new ones were just as ill-fitting as all of his others. "Well, we were warned about this in seminary—if we try too hard to please the wealthy parishioners, especially the ones who are carnally-minded, we will quickly lose the focus of bringing Christ to the lost. Or rather, bringing Christ to the ones who are actually seeking Him."

"Yes," the bishop agreed. "A crisis of complacency."

"I was literally drowning in the cares of the world and in indulgence. It was a slow drowning. It didn't happen, as you would suspect, when I first left Delta City. It began, rather, when I left St. Michael's and then worsened after my second assignment in Delta City."

The bishop just sat in silence so that Edward would continue.

"If you recall, it was that young deacon who requested my transfer from St. Michael's. For some reason, smoking cigarettes was the worst of all sins to him. I was smoking a lot then, I admit. That deacon kept on me about how the people in Meadowbrook have always been very focused on nutrition and health—he must have turned a blind eye to all the recreational drug use going on, but I digress. My hasty departure from Delta City, not to mention my task of overseeing the new church building in Meadowbrook, had increased my habits of smoking and drinking. But, despite my vices, I was still invested in reaching those 'poor in spirit' at that parish. We had an active soup kitchen there, and a radio program, and it all reminded me of my days at the Pacific Garden Mission. I also enjoyed serving Mass in the hall while the new church was being built. Being pushed away from my ministry at St. Michael's is what started the drowning."

"I do remember that deacon and his zeal to be rid of you. That wasn't of God, and things did not go well at St. Michael's for a solid decade after you left. The next priest left a black mark for some time." Bishop James shook his head as if to be rid of the memory. "I am thankful to report that things are well there, now, with an active soup kitchen again. Our Lord was speaking earnestly, of course, when he gave great importance to offering food and drink to others in His name. St. Teresa said that she always imagined each person as Jesus Himself, saying, 'I thirst.'"

"I love that," Father Edward responded before explaining. "When I arrived in Pine Valley, at St. Clement's, there were no homeless to speak of, unless you counted the war protestors, and, subsequently, there was no soup kitchen," Edward continued. "Sorry to sound so dramatic, but the only thing to welcome me was a church, only sparsely populated and only with pampered flesh. This was not good for my mental health, and my bad habits increased. I wanted to dust off my shoes and move on immediately, but that wasn't possible. Originally, I had come west from Ohio to be a missionary priest, but coming here had felt like going back to Rome."

"I am sorry, Edward," the bishop said. "But these are the types of situations where my hands are tied. I am fortunate to be in Delta City, where I can still go and be with the homeless as often as I find the time. What I am hearing, however, is that things have taken a positive turn for you. Your perseverance is paying off. I look forward to seeing how the

Lord will use you right where you are. In the meantime, what should I do about Mrs. Pedigraw and Alice?"

Edward laughed, "Thankfully, that is your job and not mine. I doubt Mrs. Pedigraw will be jumping ship too quickly. I have often heard how she despises the decorations at St. John's and the number of free-range, loud children. It would take much more to drive her there. Maybe you can tell her and Alice both that sobriety isn't easy and that I need a little space?"

"That may work," Bishop James nodded. "Edward, I really don't like to bring this other matter up, so forgive me, but there was also a report of you being seen with a young girl."

Edward sighed, "That's ok. There is no reason for concern, but I know how that must look. Margaret lives behind the rectory, and her family situation is difficult. They don't seem to mind that Margaret sneaks out at all hours. I have tried many times to shake her, but she always finds me. I will be the first to tell you that I did accept an invitation to their house for dinner. Margaret is a very perceptive child and, if the Lord has His hand in this, I want to see it through. I will tell Margaret that I will visit her entire family more often if she stops following me."

"Well, you have made me curious for sure," the bishop replied. "Please phone me as soon as you can after the dinner, and please be careful."

Bishop James stood and hugged Edward, "I must be going. I will pray for your dinner, and please pray for my trip to Alturas. I will look forward to our next visit."

"Thank you for your time and for your prayers, Your Excellency. I will walk you to your car."

As they walked toward the car, Edward couldn't help but notice what looked like a feeding frenzy of women outside of the parish hall—Mrs. Pedigraw among them. He suddenly felt drained. He remembered that the women were hosting a fundraiser for Mt. St. Paul's, the school across the street from St. Clement's.

Edward retreated to the rectory for a short rest and to think over his homily. Freed from the bondage to his addictions, Edward felt new enthusiasm when it came to his homilies. He knew that prayer was vital to his ability to offer inspiration and hope to his congregants. Prayer would even be the focus of his homily for the week from the 18th chapter of St. Luke. Brother Lawrence encouraged prayer throughout the entire day and through every task. If Brother Lawrence could have such peace and discipline while being handicapped, and washing dishes day in and day out, how much more should Edward devote himself to prayer as a shepherd of a flock?

In St. Luke, the tax collector could not even look to Heaven but, instead, implored God to have mercy upon him, 'a sinner.' Edward had taken to begging God for His mercy repeatedly for much of his walk to Dochero, as well as when he tried to fall asleep at night. Maybe his soul had once been drowning itself with self-pity and addictions, and now was satisfied instead to drown itself with his need for mercy.

Edward opened his Brother Lawrence book and read one of his prayers out loud:

> "My God, you are always close to me.
> In obedience to you, I must now apply myself to outward things.
> Yet, as I do, I pray that you will give me the grace of your presence.
> And to this end, I ask that you will assist my work, receive its fruits as an offering to you, and all the while direct all my affections to you."

"I need the grace of your presence, dear Father," Edward emphasized. "I am sorry for trying to live without it. Please bless the work of my hands for your sake."

On impulse, Edward opened his nightstand drawer and grabbed the arrowhead. He thought maybe he would take it to Dochero and throw it in the creek—be done with it forever. He traced the scar on his arm where he had once used the arrowhead as a source of punishment.

"No," he decided. "I will keep it as a reminder lest I forget that I am the chief of sinners."

He set it back in the drawer by the wooden elephant and closed it.

Edward was anxious for Wednesday to arrive, but he prayed over his tasks in the meantime.

Surprisingly, even confession had brought him a newfound sense of peace.

Edward had taken to spending more time talking with the penitent. He used to be all business, as if checking it off his to-do list. Now, after listening and praying, he would try to offer words of encouragement and comfort or spend more time allowing the person to talk. If Edward found his old annoyance bubbling up, he would silently pray for the person or ask for mercy for himself. More often now, the penitent would give themselves over to tears, and Edward knew this was healthy for them. It felt good to be helpful.

Wednesday evening came, and it seemed like Alice was getting ready for a funeral procession. Did Edward hear a "tsk, tsk" as he walked past her in the kitchen? He had been sure to tell Alice that the bishop knew of his plans and had approved them. He wouldn't have put it past Alice to spy on them this evening. Those little houses out back had thin walls.

"Let the old girl have her fun," Edward thought to himself.

He walked past the lilac bush and the driveway and pulled open the small, sagging gate that led to Margaret's small yard.

Margaret rushed out to him and grabbed his hand. Sure enough, Edward glanced back and saw Alice watching from the backdoor step, shaking her head.

Edward turned back toward the house and let Margaret pull him along.

Margaret's mother stood there at the doorway with a dignified air about her. Her dress was plain but clean, and her hair was neatly pulled back. She did not offer a smile but said, "Welcome, Father. My name is Anne, and that is my husband, Matthew." She gestured toward the table in the corner of the kitchen.

Matthew did not stand but offered a little nod before saying, "This is little Andrew." Edward's eyes adjusted to the dark, and then he saw the small boy seated at his father's side in a booster seat, fashioned with a brace. It looked as if the boy relied on the brace to keep him upright. His face was ashen and still, but his eyes were bright with expression. He did not speak and looked to be seven or eight years old—too old for a booster seat.

The house that could light up the neighborhood with noise was surprisingly quiet. The only noise was an occasional whimper coming from the back room where they must have corralled the dog.

The smells in the house were welcoming. Just ordinary smells, as you would expect from an old house with a family. It smelled like his grandmother's house on his father's side. Barely any money, but they had togetherness. Edward could never become accustomed to the artificial scents people tried to use to mask the smells of life itself.

"The chicken smells amazing," Edward offered.

"Well, sit down, then. We have a lot to talk about." Anne commanded.

Edward was taken aback but quickly took a chair. Margaret's expression was that of someone who possessed special knowledge, and she looked excited.

Anne continued, "Margaret told us about your Dochero. How did you know about it?"

"I'm not sure what you mean," Edward said, confused. "I just stumbled on it one day when I went out for a walk."

"What about the name?" Anne retorted.

"The name just came to me. My cousin and I used to have hideaways with random names."

"That's impossible," Anne said, her voice rising. "You must have heard. That girl used to call it her Dochero."

Edward was feeling very uneasy now and wondered if there had ever been a plan to eat. This felt more like an inquisition.

"I don't understand, what girl?" Edward managed.

Matthew spoke up now, still looking grim. "That quiet girl who went to Mt. St. Paul's across the way."

"Just spit it out!" Margaret said, slamming her hands onto the table. She looked across to Edward as if she was looking into his soul. "Her name was Christine."

Chapter 12

It had only been twelve weeks since Christine had arrived at Mt. St. Paul's and, already, almost half of the boarders had been kicked out. Christine started to wonder whether those girls came from family backgrounds much harder than her own. It was horrifying to imagine, really. After each departure, an unsettled feeling fell over the school, and it took days for the students to recover. If it weren't for Christine's early mornings on her knees in the chapel, it would have been impossible for her to maintain any sense of schedule or calm after each traumatic departure.

An early frost had robbed autumn of its beauty, and autumn was Pine Valley's crowning jewel. The same week that the cold temperatures snuck in, followed by freezing rains, one girl's departure had also robbed Christine of her peace. That girl, Julie, had been so full of life and fun. She called herself "Tank" and really stood out from the other girls by wearing her hair in a ducktail style. More than once, she had jumped on a table with a mock microphone to sing "He's So Fine" and do a dance, in an effort to liven up her fellow boarders. When Julie was kicked out, she went home and immediately committed suicide. It all happened so fast, and the shock of it seemed to hang on Christine like a shroud—like the same chilling, grey shroud that had snuffed out the beauty of the autumn trees.

And, to make things much worse, the president had just been shot. Christine would never forget that moment when Sister Mary Rita interrupted lunch hour with the news. Christine and her mother had adored President Kennedy. If it wasn't for Patrick, the whole family would have met the president when he came to Northern California to dedicate the Whiskeytown Dam. A family friend had invited the family to meet him, but Patrick, a Republican, had declined. Patrick had said, "I wouldn't walk across the street to meet that S.O.B."

Christine was surprised that her mother, a Democrat, had given in to Patrick rather than insisting on her way. Teresa had already picked out outfits for each of them for the occasion. Teresa wasn't the only woman who had been smitten with their president, and Patrick was probably jealous. It infuriated Patrick that Teresa was a part of the opposing party. When Patrick was gone, Teresa would often laugh about how she canceled out his vote. She had to begrudgingly host Nixon for dinner when he was running for California Governor. When Nixon's wife, Pat, asked for Teresa's scalloped potato recipe, Teresa left out a key ingredient while copying it. Nixon made eye contact with Teresa before he left and whispered to her, "I know you don't like me."

Teresa wrote to Christine immediately after President Kennedy's death and had sent along a poem she wrote about him that same day. Always a fan of Walt Whitman and "O Captain, My Captain," Teresa had used it as inspiration. "My mother is so talented," Christine thought as she was moved to tears over her mother's poem—

"The smiling faces and the outstretched hands said,
'You are ours' for these few hours
But fate says, 'You are mine.'
The stain that spread was the same bright red as the rose that fell to the floor.
From an outraged world came an anguished cry
The cry became a din.
'We love this man!' the echoes came from every shade of skin.
The caisson is gone
The riderless horse has faded into the gloom
Pray God, there please be no more room for prejudice or hate
But give us a star like the one that was stilled on his welcome to the Lone Star state."

In the midst of her grief over first Julie and then their President, the memory of another difficult loss and the comfort she received was Christine's only hope for recovering her peace.

She was twelve years old, and her hometown was similarly gripped by an early winter. Christine's mother never allowed for prolonged melancholy or inactivity, and on that particular day, she had taken Christine skiing on Cedar Pass. After half a dozen runs, they went to the small hut to have hot chocolate by the wood stove. A local man approached them and started talking about Christine's young friend, who had recently succumbed to cancer after a long battle.

"Georgia was simply an angel," he said. "It makes me angry when young people like her have to suffer."

When he walked off, Christine asked her mom if they could go home. On the ride back, Christine remembered feeling chilled to the bone, and the hot chocolate had given her a stomachache. She was consumed with thoughts of Georgia's early death—Christine had thought that death was only for old people. Georgia had been perfect, and Christine felt guilty for having envied the way all the kids had adored Georgia for her kindness and beauty—even Francis had admitted to having a crush on her.

Christine, in the back seat, stared at the pom-pom on top of her mom's ski hat. It was bouncing while Teresa dramatically belted out her favorite Mahalia Jackson gospel song, "The Old Rugged Cross"—trying to imitate Jackson's voice.

"Mom?" Christine whispered. Teresa didn't hear her. Christine raised her voice, probably for the first time in her life. "Mom, would you please be quiet? I don't feel well, and if you don't stop the car, I might throw up." As her mom slowed the car to pull over, Christine added quietly, "It came over me so suddenly—I think I'm afraid of dying."

Teresa stopped the car and turned around to face Christine, "You know what, Chrissy? I think I will take you down to see a priest in Delta City, and you can tell him about your fears."

Teresa's look of concern and her words brought relief to Christine—even though she wondered why they had to drive all the way to Delta City when they had a priest in Alturas. It was embarrassing how often they drove to Delta City. Many of her friends had never been further than Klamath Falls,

Oregon, if they had even traveled outside of the county at all. Her family seemed to go to Delta City every chance they could. "Why do we have to go all the way to Delta City?" Christine asked.

Teresa smiled and replied with a song,

"My bones denounce the buckboard bounce, and the cactus hurts my toes. Let's vamoose where gals keep usin' those silks and satins and linen that shows. And I'm all yours in buttons and bows. Gimme eastern trimmin' where women are women. In high silk hose and peek-a-boo clothes and French perfume that rocks the room, and I'm all yours in buttons and bows, buttons and bows, buttons and bows."

Christine groaned inside and thought, "Oh no, that Dinah Shore song again." That had to be one of her most embarrassing moments—when Teresa was the head of the talent show committee at Christine's school. Thinking it was just going to be the students in the talent show, Christine was shocked to see her mother, with huge puffed sleeves on her dress and a ruffled sleeping cap on her head, doing a solo rendition of "Buttons and Bows." Teresa was the only adult who performed in the show, and Christine had given her the silent treatment for a week.

Teresa stopped singing and replied, "You all need clothes anyway, so visiting the priest down there is a good excuse to go shopping."

As with every trip, Teresa assessed all the kids' clothing, made her shopping list, donned her best outfit, and then drove off with a smile. There was usually a paycheck from a fashion show waiting for her down in the city. Christine's family always stayed at the same motel on the way down, but that time, Christine felt strange being there without her siblings. It was too cold to swim, and even the promise of a hamburger and milkshake had lost its appeal.

They left the hotel early the next morning and drove to the Holy Family Catholic Church, taking a slight detour so Teresa could point out the two houses they had lived in when the children were young. Christine thought that the house closest to the church was the most charming little house she had ever seen. She cherished the thought of the cozy, simple life she had once shared with just her mother and brothers there—the trellis of roses framing the front door.

Teresa pulled to a stop in the parking lot near the parish office and then turned to face Christine. She spit a little on her hand and smoothed out Christine's bangs. Christine wilted a little under this attention. It made her feel like her looks were the most important thing.

"There," her mother had said. "Just smile and please don't fidget or pick at your lips. I am sure Father Edward will be able to help you with your fears."

Father Edward? Christine thought to herself. That was the name of a priest she remembered from long ago—one of her earliest childhood memories. Her mother was holding her after Mass, and Christine recalled reaching her arms out to a priest named Edward. Teresa had kept a tight hold on her and had not allowed her to go to him. It was as if she could still feel the pressure of Teresa's grip on her legs.

Teresa slammed her car door, bringing Christine back to the present. She got out and shyly followed behind her mother as she sailed through the door to the parish office.

"Susan, we need to speak to Father Edward."

Was it Christine's imagination, or did Susan choke a little before saying, "Well, I will have to look at his schedule. The last I looked, he was booked all day."

"No need," Teresa said. "I'll go find him."

She grabbed Christine's hand and pulled her along. "Pick up your feet," Teresa commanded. "And stand up straight."

Teresa opened a door and pulled Christine through.

Christine saw a man sitting at a desk speaking with the priest, who must have been Father Edward. The other man looked startled, but the priest remained calm.

"What is the meaning of this?" The man demanded. "You can't just barge in here unannounced."

"It's ok, Owen." The priest said. "Do you mind waiting outside for a few moments?"

Owen sighed loudly and went out the door. Teresa closed it behind him.

The priest gave them a tired smile before saying, "How may I help you, Mrs. Murphy…I mean, Mrs. Harrison?"

Teresa cleared her throat. "Chrissy, I mean Christine, needs to speak with you. She had a young friend die recently, and she has expressed some fears about death. I thought there could be no one better to talk to her than you."

"I would be honored to. It might be better if you leave us then?" He replied.

Again, Christine thought that the priest looked tired. She began to pick nervously at her lips. All she could think about was needing her Carmex, but she had left it in the car. Teresa left, firmly shutting the door.

"Hello, I am Father Edward. It has been some years since I last saw you, and you have really grown. I am sorry to hear about your friend, Christine. Do you want to tell me about her?" His eyes were kind behind his dark-rimmed glasses, and he used his finger to push them back up his nose.

"Her name was Georgia, and she was in my class," Christine told him. She kept her hands clasped tightly in her lap and tried to ignore her chapped lips. "She was so beautiful, and everyone adored her, even the boys. She had cancer for so long that I never considered that she might suddenly die from it."

"Cancer is such a tragic part of this world, and we can never quite predict how it will act. I am so sorry that you had to suffer that loss. Do you know what I think?" Father Edward asked.

Christine slowly shook her head.

"You all adored Georgia and thought she was beautiful because you saw God in her. Do you know that all people are made in God's image?" He didn't wait for an answer but continued. "For some people, it is hidden by the masks they wear. Maybe they are sad, angry, ashamed, or scared. We can cover up God's image in many ways. But Georgia wasn't wearing any masks. It sounds like she must have had joy and peace, and looking at her was like looking at Heaven itself. It doesn't sound like Georgia was scared. If she were, she would have been wearing a mask. You see, the more we let God in, the more He shines through, and I think Georgia was radiant with the love of God."

God is wherever you let God in. There was that phrase again, Christine thought.

"But why would God let her die, if she was so good?" Christine surprised herself by asking.

"Sometimes God takes His children while they are still unmarred by the world. Georgia was rescued from the broken world before it had time to put its masks on her. You know what I see in you, Christine?"

It looked like Father Edward had tears in his eyes.

"I see a young girl who is wrestling with questions. You have noticed the broken things of the world, and that is good. You are perceptive. Seeing the world as broken reminds you that you were made for something better. You were made for perfection. Some people don't notice it at all. They seem to fit right in and get comfortable in the brokenness. It is very good that you are not comfortable in it. Have you prayed about it before?"

Christine saw a tear slide beneath the rim of his glasses. He wiped it away quickly and pushed his glasses back up. Christine shook her head.

"May I pray with you?" he asked, reaching his hand across the table. "Do you want to take my hand?"

Christine just looked at his hand for a moment, unsure of what to do. He had long fingers, and if a hand could be kind, then it looked like a kind hand. She wanted to put hers there, inside his, but she was so nervous. He must have been anxious, too, because after a moment, he fidgeted with his fingers a bit before withdrawing his hand. His glasses seemed to be slipping constantly, too. He must be a smoker, Christine thought. Even her meticulous mother used to fidget like that if it had been too long since her last cigarette. That was before the Surgeon General had come out with the dangers of smoking, and Teresa had quit cold turkey.

As soon as Father Edward withdrew his hand, Christine regretted not taking it. She was surprised at her own voice then.

"Father Edward? I do want to hold your hand. May I?" She laid her hand on the table in front of him, and she saw another tear. He looked at her hand momentarily and then laid his large hand over it. He smiled at her.

Christine felt very secure in that moment. And that was the moment she would later recall when she faced tragic situations. Her hand in his.

"Dear Heavenly Father," he said. She noticed Father Edward didn't cross himself first. "Thank you for bringing Christine here today. We are saddened over the loss of her beautiful friend, Georgia, but we trust that there are no accidents with you. Death doesn't look the same to you as it does to us. Precious in your sight is the death of your saints. Yet, you did weep over the death of Lazarus. Thank you for caring about our pain—you care about Christine's. Please comfort her, Lord, and help her to make sense of it, that your understanding would become her understanding. Keep Christine pure in this life, even when brokenness comes her way. Draw her near to you at all times, Lord, and protect her. May she bring all her worries to you. In your name we pray, Jesus. Amen."

"Thank you," Christine whispered.

Father Edward took back his hand, removed his glasses, and wiped his face with a handkerchief. He left the glasses off, and Christine took a long look at his face. He reached out for her hand again.

"May God bless you, Christine." He kept hold of her hand a moment longer and used his other hand to make the sign of the cross over her. "In the name of the Father, and of the Son, and of the Holy Spirit, Amen. Would it be ok if I remember you in my prayers?"

She nodded.

Teresa walked in, and Father Edward straightened, releasing Christine's hand and grabbing for his glasses.

"I do hope you will remember her in your prayers," Teresa said. "I also hope you will remember me, too."

Christine saw the priest's countenance change, and he looked uncomfortable.

"Chrissy—I mean Christine—tell Father Edward thank you. We need to get to Neiman Marcus while it is still open." She waved a check in the air and laughed before saying, "And it is our good fortune that I just got my paycheck!"

Teresa turned to Chrissy then and lowered her voice, "Will you please go wait for me in the car? I'll be a few more minutes."

As Christine walked out, she heard Father Edward say, "That was sweet of you to bring Christine here."

Teresa replied, "I am not sweet, but I can be nice." Then she laughed.

Hearing that, Christine practically ran to the car. She opened the door and jumped in before frantically digging around in her bag for her Carmex. Then she turned the key so that her Gene Autry 8-track tape would play. Christine felt as if she had been forced to wake from a dream into the suffocating reality of hours of shopping closing in around her.

It would take years to digest that moment in time with Father Edward. Maybe it was Julie's tragic death, and the President's, or something about her time at Mt. St. Paul's, especially the early morning chapel hour on her knees, which made the memory of that comforting moment with Father Edward and the events surrounding it come into complete focus. Christine recalled how her mother had acted so strangely.

When Teresa pulled out of the parking lot that day and headed toward the mall, Christine turned down the radio and asked, "Mom, why did you bring me to see Father Edward rather than Father Sullivan back home?"

Teresa peered over a moment at Christine and said, "Father Edward was a friend of the family when we lived down here. Your dad, Murph, even decided to give Anthony the middle name of Edward after him.

"Oh, wow, that is nice." Christine responded and then added, "But how come you aren't friends anymore then?"

"We are still friends, but we just don't see each other often. Life gets complicated, that's all. Now, forget about all of that. What kind of dress were you hoping to find today?"

Christine shrugged and stared out the window. Dresses were the last thing on her mind, and she tried to tune out her mom's voice as she broke into song again—

"I'm all yours in buttons and bows, buttons and bows, buttons and bows."

Chapter 13

"How can you explain that?" Margaret's father, Matthew, asked Edward after bringing up the name of the girl who had first called the hideaway by the name Dochero.

Christine.

"There is no explanation other than just coincidence, I guess." Edward shrugged. "Or some mystery of God." That wasn't a lie, Edward thought. Christine or not, Dochero had just come to him out of thin air.

"I am always suspicious of priests, and you fit the bill then, too, I guess," Matthew replied. "May we eat now, Anne?"

"If you say so, but I don't believe this miracle thing." Anne brought a tray of chicken over to the table while Margaret brought the side dishes.

"No offense, Father, but Matthew is the head of this house, and I prefer it if he says the blessing," Anne said.

Matthew began, "Dear God, you saw fit to put us in this shack behind that church, and for Margaret to catch the priest smoking. It is our weaknesses that bring us to each other and to you, God. If the priest's hideaway at the creek has some magical or miraculous power, please show us that, too. That Andrew might be healed there. Amen."

As the family began to pass the food around, Edward thought of Matthew's prayer. So that is what this is all about—they want their son to be well. Edward felt a sudden flood of love for this family. He had not felt that for quite some time, toward anyone or toward the families of his parish. They had a real need, and perhaps he could help them.

Edward tried his food before speaking up, "This is all very delicious, Anne. Thank you. I can't recall a nicer meal."

"Now you are lying again, Father Edward," Matthew said with a stern look at Edward. "We have seen you trotting off to many a dinner at one of those fine houses that line Chapel St. I am sure they fed you much fancier food than this and loaded you up with your favorite wine."

"I can't deny that they did those things, no. But those things don't make a nice meal. You asked me here tonight for your children's sake. Margaret wanted to invite me, and you wanted me to meet young Andrew, there. Then you went to all of the trouble for this meal, and it is perfect. There is nowhere I'd rather be. That is the truth. Now, please tell me a little more about Andrew."

Margaret spoke up then. "Andrew was born that way, and none of the doctors will help him."

Anne interrupted, "He needs healing, Father Edward. I grew up going to St. John's, and I loved it as a little girl. I loved hearing the organ and believing that receiving the communion would mean that Christ would live in me and help me. And I liked nothing better than to attend midnight Mass on Christmas Eve. There were a few times that it snowed on Christmas Eve, and nothing was as magical as going to Mass with the snow falling all around and the light beckoning us through the stained glass windows."

"Yes. That was the same for me, too." Edward agreed. "I grew up going to St. Benedict's in Franklin, Ohio. We lived a block away from the church. There were many icy Christmas Eves, and we did not want to go out. But then there were the nights where snow fell fresh and the air felt warmer as we walked to the church. We could hear the organ and the cantor as we drew near, and the light poured through the stained glass. It was on one of those nights that I first wanted to make room for God in my heart. Once inside the church, I never wanted to leave. On that special night when I asked God to live in me, I was sitting next to my grandmother. She was a big German woman, and my cousins and siblings would all fight to sit next to her warmth." Edward laughed.

"Tell us more, Father Edward," Margaret said.

Edward looked over and saw that Andrew's bright eyes were fixed on him with anticipation. He didn't usually talk this much when he was invited to dinner, but he felt so at ease there.

"Well, on that night, my grandmother, or Grossmama, as we called her, had beckoned over to me. 'It is your turn, Edward. Everyone get out of his way.' She made room for me and pulled me in close. I felt so important and so loved. You see, I had lost a brother before I could know him—before I was even born. I think my parents blamed me because my mother was sick during my pregnancy. Grossmama was the only one who smothered me in love and affection. She seemed to have a never-ending supply of it. Her husband, Grosspapa, was very famous and very rich. He built huge churches, including St. Benedict's. So he was very busy. While he was away overseeing projects, Grossmama always kept her door open to her children and grandchildren. So I felt very special to be singled out that night."

"What about the part of letting God come live inside you?" Margaret asked.

"Let the father speak, Margaret!" Matthew commanded. "He was working up to it."

"Well, Father Henry gave the homily that night, and he mentioned how no one in Bethlehem had room for Joseph and Mary. I think it may have been the falling snow that made Father Henry especially reminiscent that night. We had all heard the story countless times, of course, but maybe the falling snow reminded Father Henry of his childhood in Germany. He was very emotional and even shed some tears. He made up personal stories for each of the innkeepers or the others who may have refused them a room. Everyone was too busy or distracted. Or perhaps they were hardened by the world and by sin. It made me think of how my parents seemed too sad to make any room for me in their lives. Father Henry seemed to be speaking right to me. He said, 'Maybe you are the one who is searching for a place to go, and no one has offered you a room. Maybe you feel cold, tired, or hungry? Do you know that God offers you warmth, shelter, and food? He took the most humble place on earth, a lowly stable, and turned it into a haven for his own Son, who would be the Savior of the world.' Sitting next to Grossmama made me feel like I knew what he meant. I felt secure there, but knew that it wouldn't last forever. I needed something that would last forever. Father Henry continued, 'The Savior wants to come and live in you. He will light up your life with a warm fire that will burn forever and a love that will never leave. If you give him room in your heart, you will be born again. You will be that humble stable that has new life. And from that stable God's light can shine for the whole world.'"

Edward looked at Margaret and Andrew, and their little eyes were bright with anticipation. He looked at Matthew and Anne—their eyes were full of desperation and longing.

He continued, "I knew then that I just wanted to be that humble stable that took on new life. I couldn't care less about my family's wealth. I knew I would go far from them one day. If I didn't leave, I would be trapped in the same old thing, day after day, year after year. I knew I would be a priest, as they wanted, but not exactly as they imagined. I eventually learned that out west, they didn't have a lot of the massive, established, wealthy parishes. The West was a mission field, and that is where I wanted to go."

"So was it smooth sailing after that, Father? Your family's wealth still had your back. You were full of God and full of their backing. You still had it easier than us." Matthew's bitterness rose again.

"To you, it might appear that way, yes. I had everything going for me, it seemed. But, you see, this is a life of suffering we take on as priests. We must press into that suffering, and I didn't always do that. There were times that I allowed myself to be cushioned by the things of the world—dulled by them, really. Abbot Daniel said, "The more obese your body becomes, the more emaciated your soul becomes." Rich or poor, it doesn't matter—we shouldn't become dull to the way God is refining us, or spiritually emaciated. Maybe the rich are more easily trapped, I don't know. You have had great burdens, but like me, you can either take them up for the sake of Christ or become bitter about them. If you don't reach out to God in your suffering, then it is as if he hides himself from you. We each have that choice. Which way have you chosen, Matthew?"

"I don't see that as any of your business. You don't know us or the troubles of our lives." Matthew crossed his arms and challenged Edward with his eyes.

"Matthew, please," Anne implored. "We want the father to take us to his Dochero. If you won't tell him, I will." Anne turned to Edward. "We want you to take all of us to Dochero and baptize Andrew there, so that he might be healed."

Edward looked at all of their eyes again and knew that he couldn't say no. He collected his thoughts for a moment before asking, "Is this what you want, Andrew?"

Andrew smiled and nodded.

"That is very unconventional, and I imagine many wouldn't approve. However, I don't want to limit God's power. I will ask the bishop for his permission, but not announce it to the parishioners. Bishop James is kind and understanding. For everyone else, I will just call it a field trip to the old mining site. My housekeeper, Alice, might fret about it if she thinks we are breaking a church law or something of that sort. Shall we meet at the rectory then?"

Matthew pushed back from the table and stood. "We will see you there a week from this Saturday, first light. It is time for the kids to go to bed. Goodnight."

Anne nervously extended her hand, "Thank you for coming, Father Edward."

"Thank you for having me. Nice to meet you all."

As Edward stepped out the door, Margaret grabbed his hand, as if to walk all the way with him.

Edward bent low to speak with her, but spoke loud enough for all to hear as he pushed his glasses back up his face. "Margaret, I need to ask a favor. I would love to spend time with your whole family now that I have met them. But we need to make a deal. You can't come and find me anymore or single me out. That raises suspicion among the people. If we are going to spend time together, it has to be with your whole family. Will you agree to that?"

Margaret looked crestfallen but nodded her head and replied, "I guess. It seems I can never keep anything to myself in this world, but if it will help Andrew, then I will agree to that."

"Very well and thank you. Good night." Edward removed his hand and walked across the alley. He impulsively turned around when he reached his back steps. "Margaret, are you still there? There is one thing you can keep all to yourself, and that is your talks with your heavenly Father. Your prayer life is all your own, and no one can ever take that from you." He thought he could hear a sniffle from Margaret in reply.

"How did it go, Father?" Alice accosted him the moment he came through the back door. Edward jumped. "Are they just as loud inside as they are from the outside?"

Edward figured Alice had been spying and already knew the answer to that question. "In brief, Alice, I would say the evening was very refreshing—refreshingly quiet. Good night." Edward continued to his room and shut the door firmly.

He sat on his bed to process everything. Without the crutches of wine and cigarettes, he had found that he needed to do that—give himself time to think, and feel, and just be still. After a time, a memory came from an evening that resembled the one he had just had. It had been an evening of pure bliss, and it happened when he first went to the Delta City Diocese.

There had been a different bishop at the time—Bishop Brown. Bishop Brown had helped him settle into the Holy

Family Catholic Church Parish and the rectory when Edward first came west. Part of his duty as a young priest was to train the altar servers. It was a thankless task at times, as most of the boys were forced to serve by their parents. There was, however, one boy who was a joy to work with. His name was Francis. Francis was Irish, and he reminded Edward of some of his Irish friends in seminary. His wit and humor were mature for his age. He seemed happy to get away from home to serve, and he frequently signed up. Francis told Edward that his father was an angry drunk, and he got away at every opportunity. He had a younger brother, Joseph, and his mother was very pregnant with her third child.

Francis would normally walk over for Mass, but on one particularly stormy day, his mother drove him. Edward had just walked out of the rectory when they pulled up.

His mother rolled down her window and called out, "You must be Father Edward? I am Teresa, or Mrs. Murphy, I should say, Francis's mom."

Mrs. Murphy's smile was captivating, and her laugh even more so. "We live close, but even I need an excuse to get out once in a while. The rain was my chance. I'll go park the car, and I'll see you at Mass."

Edward hadn't said a word, but he already felt sick, knowing that poor Mrs. Murphy was married to an angry drunk. He hadn't recalled ever meeting such a lively young woman—save his cousin, Gigi, maybe.

It was tough for Edward to focus on Mass that day, but he had implored the Lord for mercy over and over again in his mind. Thankfully, he was only assisting—since he wasn't allowed to do Mass alone yet.

After Mass, he received his first dinner invitation from Mrs. Murphy. "My husband will love you. Most of his friends are priests," she had said. She added with a laugh, "I think he was meant to be a priest, but he got off track when he met me."

Edward should have known to steer clear after that comment, but that evening would become the first of many dinners.

Those dinners were pure bliss, and his night at Margaret's reminded him of them in some ways. The dinners with the Murphy family were very simple. Most of their money was being drained by Mr. Murphy's bottles, but Mrs. Murphy was very good at making do. She washed all their clothing and linens by hand—without a washing machine. She even mowed the lawn and repurposed furniture.

You could tell the family was very close, especially the mother and her boys. The humor and wit were inherited traits. Whereas Edward's own family had walls built between them, the only walls at Margaret's house or the Murphys' were the ones built around the family as a whole. And both families had chosen to let Edward in.

As he sat in his room that night, a troubling thought entered his mind. He had just agreed to do something with Margaret's family that the church would frown upon. The church had also frowned upon his too frequent visits to the Murphys' house. He opened the drawer and grabbed the arrowhead. He clenched it so tightly that he knew there would be blood.

Edward lay on his bed and implored God for His mercy. The purpose he had felt at dinner that night had already fled. He wanted to help Margaret's family, but wondered if it would lead to his destruction. He threw the arrowhead against the wall and started to weep.

"Please draw near to me, God. Don't hide yourself. Guide me. Please, God, help."

Edward heard soft knocking on his door. "Father Edward? Are you alright?" Alice asked. "May I get you something?"

Edward composed himself and sat up. "No, that's alright. Everything is fine. Good night, Alice."

"Good night, Father Edward." Edward listened for her footfall as she walked away.

Edward felt oddly comforted by Alice's voice and her quiet sounds.

"God bless her," Edward said. "Forgive me, Lord, for my evil thoughts toward her. Please help her and her son, Buddy, to find their way."

Edward wiped the blood off his hand, dropped to the ground, and began his prostrations.

Chapter 14

Besides bringing back memories from long ago, Julie's untimely death pushed Christine into a new season of life. The memory of Father Edward was very clear in her mind and was producing some juxtaposing results. Father Edward's words about death were very comforting. Like with Georgia, she didn't believe that a loving God would have abandoned Julie in her last hours. Julie's life had always been hard, and maybe the world was too much for her. The broken world, as Father Edward had said. Perhaps she wanted to be with God and be done with it all. Who could fault her for that? No, Christine reprimanded herself. She knew suicide was very wrong, and she would just have to trust that God would work out all those details.

The other result from that memory was the way Christine thought about her mother. This first time of separation had already given Christine a different perspective on her family, but now she was really beginning to wonder.

Why had Teresa driven her all the way to Delta City to see Father Edward when they could have just gone to see Father Sullivan? It was no secret they all wished Father Sullivan would just go back to Ireland, but he was nice enough. There had been some scandal—she wasn't sure what it was, but it wasn't anything that affected Christine's family. Surely, as a priest, he was equipped to comfort a child about death.

Christine recalled walking up to the open casket at Georgia's funeral. Georgia looked as beautiful and as peaceful as always. Father Sullivan stood next to Georgia's father, and he motioned for Christine after she had viewed the body. When Christine approached them, Georgia's father said, "You were Georgia's closest friend." Then he broke down into sobs and grabbed Christine into an embrace. She felt like she would be crushed before Father Sullivan gently removed her from Georgia's father's arms.

"There, there," Father Sullivan said, "You are a great comfort, Christine. One of God's precious lambs. So like Georgia."

That had frightened her a little. Maybe she would be the next one to go if she were one of God's precious lambs.

Perhaps that is why her mother had sought out a different opinion. Either way, her mother's demeanor was odd at the Holy Family Catholic Church in Delta City. Teresa had sprayed on extra perfume in the car and then marched right down the hall to Father Edward's office.

Maybe this season of life meant she was becoming a woman. Christine was becoming her own person, and she keenly felt the distance from her mother. She didn't want to duplicate Teresa's smug attitude or her mischievous ways. Christine didn't want to put on airs or treat others heartlessly.

She recalled poor Mr. Gibson, who lived next door to Christine's family. He had recently been widowed and had grown increasingly grumpy. Teresa made fun of him constantly, and Christine's older brothers seemed to eat up the humor. Without his wife, the only thing Mr. Gibson seemed to know how to do with his time was chop wood. As the wood piles grew in his front yard, Teresa started calling him the local wood rat. She would say, "He acts as if he were to stop cutting wood, he would die." Then something happened that was the last straw.

Christine's older brother, Joseph, had taken an internship with the Forest Service and spent his summers in the outdoors conducting surveys. The summer before, he had come upon a gravely injured and very pregnant porcupine. He had to put her out of her misery, and then he and his work friends decided to cut her open and take out her porcupette. Christine's family welcomed "Yogi" as their pet. The whole family grew very fond of Yogi as they nursed him to maturity. He was king of the house and could go in and out as he pleased. One day, Yogi wandered into Mr. Gibson's yard and, not knowing it was a pet, Mr. Gibson did what most people in Modoc would do—he hit the porcupine over the head with a shovel and killed him. The family was, of course, devastated, and Teresa saw this as a declaration of war.

The next morning, Teresa said, "The jig is up." She then posted an ad in the paper that said "Free Wood, You Load and You Haul." Of course, the address listed was Mr. Gibson's. Christine will never forget the forlorn look she saw on Mr. Gibson's face as half a dozen trucks and trailers pulled up and people began to load up all of his wood. He walked around with that same shovel but was too dazed to do more than wave it around. People ignored him and just kept loading.

Teresa and the boys were delighted, and they treated the event like a spectator sport. "Chrissy, can you make us more popcorn?"

Looking back, Christine felt like a built-in spectator to Teresa's big personality. The world revolved around Teresa and the importance she placed on maintaining a good image. Retreating to her room and to her prayers was Christine's solace. Leaving for Mt. St. Paul's was the opportunity she had been waiting for.

Sister Mary Rita had wasted no time in asking both Christine and Nancy if they would consider the religious life. They were still the only two girls who attended morning chapel. Sister Mary Rita's question, along with Julie's tragic death, gave Christine and Nancy a lot to think about. Contemplating a life of conformity sent them into a season of non-conformity.

The girls had taken to sneaking off campus after dinner, when the nuns were enjoying their moments of respite. The old mining site, with its wooden bridges, dense foliage, and rushing stream, drew the girls like a magnet. They weren't interested in boys yet, although Nancy told Christine that all the boys liked her. "If we were allowed to date, they would probably ask you out," Nancy suggested on that first walk to the mining site. "But you never smile and are so shy. What's with that?"

"I have no interest in going out with a boy, not yet anyway. My brothers always warn me about becoming a flirt. 'Never smile at the boys or you will give them the wrong impression,' they say. I like being alone, and I might be suited to become religious. What about you? Do you think you will want to be a nun?"

"It's hard to say," Nancy replied. "I want to live a little first. I do want to go out with a boy. I am very curious about them. I don't have a million brothers like you do or a dad. My dad walked out on my mom when she was pregnant with me."

"Oh!" Christine exclaimed. "I am so sorry."

They walked in silence for a while, and Christine considered what that must be like—just Nancy and her mom, no boys around. But I don't really have a dad either, Christine thought. After the divorce was final, Christine had never seen her dad again. Christine had no memory of him whatsoever. He sent Christmas presents each year—maple sugar candy, Lifesaver candy, storybooks, and boxes of random toys and trinkets. Teresa said he had taken to inventing games, and he sent them his prototypes. Her mother said, "It's always the same ol', same ol'—just a bunch of crapola. He never puts a moment of thought into those gifts. Murph doesn't know his own kids and that's that."

Patrick was not a dad to Christine either. Blood was everything to him, but she didn't want to steal the show from Nancy by telling her so. And it was true that Christine was very fortunate to have so many older brothers as makeshift dads. They really did watch out for her. She recalled Anthony punching her in the arm when she forgot to set the parking brake after a driving lesson. The Jeep had rolled down the hill into Mr. Gibson's garage door. After he punched her in the arm, he said, "And this is so you will remember never to do that again."

Walking into the area below the old mining site for the first time felt like entering a dense jungle. It was so unlike the high desert country Christine was accustomed to. Nancy was from a desolate part of Nevada, so she was also taken aback by the stark contrast.

They ran down the path and onto the bridge, stopping in the middle to peer down at the creek below. "I'll race you to the bottom!" Nancy challenged her, running off before Christine could even answer.

Christine was lost entirely in the moment and didn't even hear Nancy.

"God is wherever you let God in." That old familiar phrase came back to her. It was weird to hear the phrase somewhere other than her bedroom—that sweet room with the sunshine and golden hues. Now, it was all greenery surrounding her on the bridge. Most of the light was blocked by the trees' canopy, and a mist hung in the air. Yes, she thought, God can be here, too. Not just my bedroom, or the church back home, or the chapel. He is everywhere.

A word came to her then, "Dochero."

It was a whisper of a word, and Christine had to hear it a second time before grabbing hold of it.

Dochero.

Christine remembered Nancy then, and she called out, "Nancy? Did you hear that?"

Nancy's reply sounded distant, and Christine couldn't hear her over the sound of the stream. Christine saw Nancy along the water's edge, and Christine made the descent. A worn path jutted down sharply at the end of the bridge, and Christine descended carefully.

"Did you hear that back there?" Christine asked when she met Nancy at the bottom.

"Hear what?" Nancy replied.

"I heard a word, Dochero."

"Nope, I didn't hear anything."

"It was strange. Either way, I think it is a neat word. Let's call this place our Dochero."

"Sounds good to me!" Nancy exclaimed. "This can be our hideaway as we contemplate the religious life. We also need to contemplate our report on leprosy, we have to give our speech next week!"

The girls shrieked and giggled.

Christine said, "How about we also contemplate the dinner they served us last night? Could you believe it? Graham crackers, green salad, and hot cakes! What a weird combination. And then the trusty Tang to drink. The cook seems desperate lately. I found three of her gray hairs in my food last week. I wrote home about that and about how the heater seems broken, so we freeze at night. I signed my letter, Christine, Mt. St. Paul's, Home for Wayward Girls."

The girls laughed again.

"All of these grievances are adding up, and I'm starting to formulate a plan," Nancy offered. "As you know, the one hundredth anniversary of Mt. St. Paul's is coming up, and I think all of the school's money and efforts have gone into the preparations, not the food. It has been two weeks since we have had hot water! They don't want to spend money to repair the water heater. The anniversary celebration is all that the teachers and the principal are talking about—not to mention the big committee."

Christine and Nancy had refused to join the committee. Their failure to join, along with their habit of attending chapel, had given the committee girls another reason to ostracize them.

"I think I have an idea of how to add our own contribution to the celebration." Nancy looked at Christine with a mischievous grin.

Christine felt the old familiar dread come on, like when her mom had one of her schemes. But she couldn't let her only friend down, so she felt herself getting swept away by something beyond her control.

Chapter 15

Edward felt uneasy about taking Margaret and her family to Dochero, but he did not want to let them down. Not when they so badly needed his help. Bishop James had been so kind as to give him permission to baptize Andrew under these special circumstances.

"Sometimes we have to encourage people with the seed of faith they have. Andrew's father is looking for a miracle, and we don't want to discourage that. Don't forget that the early church preferred baptizing in natural bodies of water. In fact, I wish I could come with you, but I will be up in Alturas again."

During Mass on Sunday, Edward was surprised to see Margaret's family make their way into the church about fifteen minutes late. Edward noticed the annoyance on people's faces at the late newcomers. He silently prayed that someone would make room for them. Most parishioners sat in the same pews each Sunday, and Edward often thought to himself that those people acted like it would be a mortal sin to give up their pews to someone else. "What is wrong with them?" he asked himself.

Alice looked shocked rather than annoyed when she saw the family, and Edward tried to maintain good thoughts towards her. Bonnie was the only one to offer a welcoming smile to the family, and she motioned for them to sit next to her. Matthew had a look of resolve on his face as he shuffled into the pew carrying Andrew, stiff as a board, in his brace. Margaret looked very pleased with herself, and Anne looked nervous.

Edward had felt unusually tired that morning, but, as always, he was thankful he had pushed through—knowing that God would meet him in the liturgy, as he had countless times before.

Christ in me, the hope of glory.

One of the altar servers that morning, Thomas, with a twinkle in his eyes, reminded him of Francis Murphy from long ago. He resolved, once again, to push the Murphy family from his mind. They are the Harrison family now, he thought. Edward gave Thomas a smile and tried to focus. He actually appreciated moments of spontaneous humor in the pulpit— Edward believed God had a sense of humor, too. They were made in His image after all. Nothing was worse than going to a Mass that lacked joy and vitality. Edward couldn't help wondering whether certain priests were even spirit-filled. He wasn't supposed to judge, but doesn't the Bible say we will know people by their fruit? How else can we tell if someone is really in the faith? Or if they are a wolf in sheep's clothing?

Edward brought his thoughts back to the Mass and to the second reading being read by Lector Phillip. It was almost time for the Gospel reading and his homily. When he was preparing earlier in the week, he never imagined that Margaret's family would be in attendance today. Edward silently prayed for wisdom as he went forward for the homily.

Edward opened by saying, "It all goes back to humility and love when it comes to our Lord and our time on this earth. It is all very simple, really. We admit our need for Him. We admit we are sinners in need of His healing and grace. He did pay for those sins once and for all on the cross, and He proclaimed 'It is finished.' That does not mean we can sit back and think we are finished, though—even after a declaration of faith or after the sacraments. It is still a daily choice to humble ourselves and to follow Him. We should be like the tax collector that we read about in St. Luke's Gospel. The tax collector was so humble, knowing his own sinfulness, that he would not look up to heaven, or even approach the temple, but rather he beat his breast and said, 'God, have mercy on me, a sinner.' Jesus spoke this parable to those who were confident of their own righteousness. Which one am I? Which one are you? Do we brag and say, 'Yes, I have believed. I am going to heaven. I confess every week?' Or rather, should we say over and over, 'Jesus, have mercy on me, a sinner?' If we aren't in tears over our sin, we are not in a position to approach our Lord. We must first stand off like the tax collector and beg Him for his healing and mercy." Edward scanned the eyes of the congregants, including Margaret's family, but was careful not to stare too long at any one face.

He continued, "We are not made to get comfortable in this life. Instead, we should approach life as ones passing through—as pilgrims. This is not our home. If you examine yourself and find yourself comfortable and complacent, it is time to start asking the Lord for answers. From there, He will always point back to humility and love. Have you humbled yourself, a sinner? Do you love your neighbor?"

Edward's eyes met those of Matthew for a moment. "Forget about even your neighbor and ask yourself if you love your own family well. If you aren't loving your own family, start there. Or rather, forget about even your family and ask yourself if you love God. If you are not loving God, start there. And there is no relationship without honesty. Be honest with your Lord. Be honest about your sin. In that honesty, there is nothing He won't forgive. In your humility and by His grace, He will help you. He will then help you love your family and love your neighbor." Edward began to hear sniffling in the congregation, and he saw people wiping their eyes. He was having a hard time keeping his own composure.

"Don't get comfortable, friends. Don't get comfortable in your same pews and be unwilling to share." Edward raised his eyebrows then and took a slow look around before continuing. "Don't be like the Pharisees—confident in their own righteousness. We are pilgrims on a journey, and the journey won't stop until we meet our Lord face to face. This is a life of constant need for healing, and this is the posture we should take—by God's grace—we are healed, we are being healed, we will be healed. Keep knocking, keep traveling, keep running the race. Lord, please help us not to be complacent. Please help us to approach all of life with humility and love. Lord, we humbly ask for your mercy, grace, and healing. In the name of the Father and of the Son and of the Holy Spirit. Amen."

Edward looked up to see Matthew wiping his cheeks and nose. Edward felt such love toward that whole family. Why did he not feel that way about the Pedigraws and most of the others? He asked for the Lord's forgiveness again before beginning preparations for the Eucharist. Despite everything over the years—his childhood, seminary, and then his great fall—Edward loved losing himself in the Liturgy of the Eucharist. All earthly cares ceased as Edward remembered that Jesus came to be the life of the world, and that He is the life of the world. Edward prayed that his congregants would come to embrace that life as their own, in repentance, and be set free from the power of sin and death.

> God, our Creator,
> may this bread and wine we offer
> as a sign of our love and worship
> lead us to salvation.
> Grant this through Christ our Lord.

Edward took more time here than other priests. That is because he had his own inward prayers between his spoken words. He wasn't sure whether it was technically correct to keep up that dialogue, but he argued that it would be wrong not to. He had to constantly ask for God's forgiveness for his wayward thoughts. They came at him like arrows during this part of the Mass. There was no explanation for some of them except that they were straight from the enemy.

Help me focus, Lord, forgive my thoughts. I am not worthy to receive you, but only say the word and my soul shall be healed.

There was no doubt that Edward was not worthy. He was glad he was in this place of humility. He hadn't been able to hide his sin, and maybe that was a good thing. Any good parent should pray that their children's sins should be found out, after all. That had not been the norm for his family growing up. Everything was hidden—hidden under layers of fine clothes, behind thick walls of finely built homes, and beneath piles of money.

Meeting Billy Sunday repeatedly while Edward was in Chicago and attending services at Pacific Garden Mission, otherwise known as the Old Lighthouse, had given Edward a new perspective.

"We are all just beggars telling other beggars how to find a piece of bread," Sunday had explained. "That is what another preacher said. You are going to be a preacher someday, too, Edward, even if that is not what they call it at your church. You are going to have the opportunity to lead another beggar to the Bread of Life. If you are going to be a good preacher, I am sorry to say that you will experience suffering of some kind—perhaps due to your own sin or someone else's. Suffering is the only way to be humbled enough that another soul will actually listen to you."

That had been scary to hear for young Edward, but he had never forgotten those words. As he stood in the pulpit holding the life-giving elements once again, begging God for forgiveness and praying for his congregants, he allowed himself to pray these words again, "God, I am not worthy, but please, God, please bless Christine and do not hold my sins against her. Sweet Jesus, please save her."

Chapter 16

"So what is our plan again?" Christine asked Nancy as they walked back into the school after another visit to Dochero on the morning of Mt. St. Paul's centennial celebration. Nancy didn't seem to notice the lack of enthusiasm in her voice.

"I'm not entirely sure yet," Nancy replied. "I know the photographers will be coming for the day to document the occasion. Maybe we can contribute to the festivities somehow." Nancy giggled and twirled, making her skirt flare.

Nancy always wore thick plaid skirts with the appropriate hem length for Mt. St. Paul's. Nancy had her best one on that day, and it made Christine think of the skirt Aunt Virginia had sent her last summer from Saks Fifth Avenue. Every morning at school, before lessons began, Mother Superior would whisk into the classroom. All the students had to immediately stand up by their desks, and then the boys were allowed to sit down. While the girls stood in place, Mother Superior would walk down the rows checking their hem lengths. One morning, soon after school started, Christine was wearing the Saks Fifth Avenue skirt, and it was too short. Mother Superior said, "That's a very nice skirt, Dear, but you need to go upstairs and change and then send the skirt home." So far, Christine had been the only girl to have to change that year.

Undaunted, Christine ran upstairs and changed. She stuffed the skirt deep into her dresser drawer with no intent of mailing it back.

"Anyone home?" Nancy asked, breaking Christine from her thoughts. They walked up the school steps, and Nancy whispered, "Live a little while you can!" She grabbed Christine's hand and yanked her through the door.

"Now that I think about it, maybe it will be fun to get back at that planning committee and all the cliquish girls who snubbed us," Christine thought to herself.

The girls ran up the stairs.

Nancy flew to the second-story window and peered out. "I see the photographers arriving. Quick, I have the perfect idea." Nancy grabbed Christine's arm and yanked her toward the stairwell. "Let's go to the third floor!"

Christine felt a rush of excitement as she followed Nancy upstairs.

"Quick, the laundry room!" Nancy exclaimed.

It was all a blur as Christine followed Nancy in. The next thing Christine knew, Nancy had opened the windows facing out onto the front lawn where the photographers were.

"Come on!" Nancy beckoned to Christine. "Help me!"

Nancy started grabbing clothing that had been set out to dry—bras and underwear in particular—and then threw them out the windows.

It was all happening so fast, and before she had even registered what was happening, Christine threw a bra out the window, too. Then she just stood there, looking down to see what the effect had been. Bras and underwear were hanging from ledges and window frames all the way down the face of the building. Then a photographer pointed up, and Christine ducked out of the way before he could get a picture of her.

"Hurry," Nancy whispered. "I think I hear Sister Mary Rita's skirts."

The girls snuck out and reached the cafeteria in time for lunch. The whole room was buzzing about the spectacle out front. "Who did it?" The girls asked each other.

Sister Mary Rita rushed through the door, flushed, and yelled, "I hope to God I never find out who did this." Then she pivoted with a swoosh of her skirts and was gone. There were too many festivities left in the day to dwell on the incident. Christine thought Nancy was being obvious in all her glee, but then Christine also knew that her own guilt must be written all over her face. She left the cafeteria when no one was looking and headed up to the dormitory. The stress immediately caused a boil to form on Christine's leg. It was so painful, but Christine knew she deserved it. "I don't have to ask if there is a wicked way in me—I know there is, and now I will pay the price. Maybe if I write a letter home, Mom will send a remedy for the boil." Christine was glad the dormitory was empty, and she knelt by her bed to pray.

"Please forgive me, Lord. I don't want to be kicked out. I love it here more than anywhere else in the world. Maybe Sister Mary Rita is right, maybe I will become a nun. Just please don't let us get caught, and I will try to avoid any more troublemaking. Please also help with this boil."

Her prayers were answered in two ways. The anniversary celebration incident was surprisingly never brought up again. Then, Christine had a surprise opportunity to stay a little longer when her freshman year drew to a close.

It was odd, really. Why had Teresa written letters to the school asking if Christine could stay longer at the end of the year, and that she couldn't afford to pay the last part of tuition? Perhaps her mother and Patrick were finally separating? When Christine had gone home to Alturas for Christmas break, there was tension between them.

Teresa didn't hide the reasons from Christine. She told her that one day, while driving back from the store, she saw Patrick outside a hotel with one of his female clients. "That's how his first marriage ended, you know. While attending Stanford University, he married a socialite. It was all over the newspapers. Then he went to war overseas and started spending time with a nurse. One day, he decided to write both his wife and the nurse letters, but, unlucky for him, he accidentally put them in the wrong envelopes. The socialite divorced him soon after. I don't think he ever got over that. He even tried calling her when we were on our honeymoon."

Christine responded with a little more spunk than usual, "Didn't you see all of that as a red flag? From what the boys said, we had a great life before Patrick came into the picture. Living in the outdoors all summer and in the French Hotel in the winter. We were happy just to have you and each other."

"Watch your mouth, you little snip!" Teresa said sharply before immediately softening. "We were basically homeless during that time. We were living off of everyone's

138

charity, and I had to leave you kids on your own to go to work at the hospital each day." Teresa grew pensive but seemed to enjoy thinking back on some of the details.

"Did you know that I used to leave a .22 rifle propped up near the hospital's back door? I was determined to shoot the next buck I saw eating from the apple tree in the nearby orchard. I wanted so bad to bring back a huge buck to show the other boarders at that hotel. There were many mornings I would sneak out at first light to hunt the hills behind the hotel. If you were awake, I would take you with me. I didn't have the papoose yet, so sometimes I would just carry you in my arms."

Teresa laughed, "Did I tell you about the time I had buck fever? I had been carrying you all over the place, as well as my gun. We crested a hill, and there was a huge buck only about 40 yards away. I set you down and grabbed the gun. My arms were either shaking so badly from carrying you all that distance, or they were shaking from buck fever. Either way, I missed that close shot. I couldn't believe it! I think you were in shock from the gunshot because you almost immediately fell asleep afterward."

"I'm sorry, I probably made you miss." Christine offered.

"Oh, don't be silly," Teresa laughed again. "I've gotten several Boone and Crockett bucks since then. I think Patrick's jealous. He's been jealous of everything since the beginning. He's jealous of my relationship with all of you kids. The last couple of pregnancies, he took me out and bounced me in the Jeep through the lava rock, hoping I would lose the babies."

Christine knew Teresa was gathering evidence for a divorce. She was planning to ask Christine to testify against Patrick in court, and Christine was dreading the day she would need to do so. She already knew Patrick disliked her. She also had guilt concerning her mom's first divorce. Was her birth the reason for that divorce? Her mother had been pregnant with her when she got divorced after all.

To be a nun would be so much easier, Christine thought. There would be no difficult men and no breakups. She would be married to God, instead.

So, no matter the cause, it came as excellent news that she could stay longer at the end of the term. It was hard to say goodbye to Nancy, however. They promised to meet once a year at Dochero for as long as they lived.

"It might not be too far-fetched if we both become nuns and work here," Nancy suggested. "We can just go to Dochero on our cigarette breaks."

They both laughed then and held each other in a long hug.

"I'll write you every week," Christine said as she pulled away.

"Oh, please do!" Nancy replied. Then she repeated part of the Mt. St. Paul's slogan as she walked away. "And don't forget after each day that 'another day is over—a busy day, but a happy day—living, working, praying, and playing together.'"

The girls had one last laugh together.

Christine saw Sister Mary Rita watching them from a distance, and she called Christine over as soon as Nancy's mom drove away.

"Is everything ok?" Christine asked as she walked over. Inside, she was thinking that she would finally get what she deserved from the anniversary incident.

"Well, I am a little concerned about your family situation, Christine. Do you know of any reason that your parents can't pay your tuition or come to get you?"

"I can't think of anything," Christine responded.

"I called the diocese and did a little research—since your family has been part of the diocese for many years."

Christine thought that Sister Mary Rita was looking at her with an odd expression.

"It sounds like the diocese will be more than happy to help with your tuition, so all is well. It is quite providential that we can keep you as a holdover for a little while. We can discuss your consideration of the religious life more seriously. Come along, Dear."

Sister Mary Rita motioned for Christine to follow her to her office. Once there, she pulled a small book from her bookshelf and extended it toward Christine.

"I think you should read this one, written by St. Teresa of Avila. It is called 'The Way of Perfection.' It will give you a lot to think about concerning the sisterhood." Sister Mary Rita opened the book to a bookmarked page. "I especially like this line here, 'Never suppose that either the evil or the good you do will remain secret, however strict may be your enclosure.'"

She gave Christine a hard look and held it for a moment.

Christine wondered why she chose that quote. It made her feel funny. Was Sister Mary Rita thinking about the incident with Nancy?

Christine remembered the time her mother said that, because of her own mischievous ways as a kid, she felt guilty even when she wasn't. Christine felt guilty all the time now. It all made Christine wonder again about generational sins and whether she was guilty of her parents' and grandparents' sins. She decided to ask Sister Mary Rita.

"May I ask you about generational sin, Mother? Am I always going to be guilty of my ancestors' sins, or did Jesus take away those sins, too?"

"It is interesting that you mention that. Why does that concern you, Christine? Most teenagers don't think about things like that."

"Well, my grandfather was a bootlegger during Prohibition. His young son died in an accident shortly after the revenuers caught up with him. That would have been my uncle."

"That is very unfortunate," Sister Mary Rita said. "What about your mother? What has she done?"

That confused Christine. What about her mother? Was it because she was divorced?

"Well, it's kind of embarrassing, but she stole Christmas trees and made me help her. She used to snitch a lot on her little brother, the one who died. I know she felt bad about that. Oh, and there was the time she made a boy drive her four hours to a party, and then she didn't even let him go in with her. That was about the time she said that her parents couldn't wait for her to move out. Is that what you mean?" Christine asked, feeling bad for saying so much about her mom.

"No, but that is all interesting. Anything else?"

Why did Christine feel like she was being interrogated about her mother? What did Sister Mary Rita know that she didn't?

"Well, I think she was named after your St. Teresa of Avila. Her mother was very pious. Why are you asking? Is my mother ok?" Christine asked, alarmed. "Is something wrong with her? Is that why I am still here? Because even though she did all of that, I know she does a lot of good, too. She has been a faithful representative of the Miraculous Medal Association for as long as I can remember. She even drives cancer patients to their appointments. And, one Thanksgiving, she went out to find as many homeless people as possible to join us for dinner. That quote you just said from Teresa of Avila said that the good won't stay a secret either. Well, when I was home for Christmas, I caught my mother praying on her knees. She was praying for a long list of people, both alive and dead. She looked so beautiful kneeling there like that." Christine was suddenly homesick for the first time, and especially for her mother.

"Calm down, Christine. I think your mother is fine. I was just thinking about what I heard from the diocese." Sister Mary Rita was patting her arm.

Christine had tuned her out, and it was in that split second that she decided that she would never be a nun. Not if she was going to be someone like Sister Mary Rita.

"Sorry to disappoint you, Nancy," Christine whispered.

Chapter 17

Edward's early mornings no longer felt so urgent and secretive. Instead, he felt a calm acceptance of the new day and all that God had in store for him. After feeding the stray cats, he had taken to stepping out to the front of the house to watch the sunrise and greet whomever he might encounter. Alice, shocked at the turn of events, had been too timid to join him at first but now brought him a cup of coffee—still in her bathrobe and curlers. She stood in the doorway so as not to be seen.

"How is Buddy?" Edward asked her one morning, as the pink streaks illumined the sky beyond them. Alice didn't look as much like a scarecrow close up, Edward thought.

"That is very kind of you to ask, Father Edward. He truly is considering the cloth and wondered if he might speak to you over the phone?"

"That would be fine. I am sorry I have neglected to do that. Would this evening work well?"

"Why, yes!" Alice sputtered. "He will be so pleased! I will mark it in your calendar right now."

"Before you go, Alice," Edward said quickly, as if he would lose his nerve. "Please make sure you have it in my calendar, for Saturday morning, to meet Margaret's family out back. We are going to go over to the old mining site together."

"Oh?" Alice hesitated. "That is the day I had taken off to spend the day with my mother in Nevada City. Are you sure you will be alright with those folks? Do you think maybe Bonnie should go with you?"

Edward teased Alice, "That's magnanimous of you to suggest including Bonnie. We are all on the same team, you know—you, me, and Bonnie against the world. However, out of all of Bonnie's amazing feats, taking long walks is not one of them."

Alice smiled despite herself. "That's true, I am the more athletic one. She could walk partway, though—it would be good for her. Would you like me to call her for you?"

"Thank you for suggesting it, but both of you ladies should enjoy your day off. Don't worry yourself about it—but please, do mark it down so I won't forget."

Transparency was new for Edward, and he liked the feeling it gave him. Another new feeling was the satisfaction Edward felt from the amount of money he was saving by not spending it on cigarettes or wine. He only occasionally accepted a glass when it was offered now. And, only in the company of other men. The money was adding up quickly, and he was wondering what he might do with it.

Not everything was easy, however, in this new life with no hang-ups. Like in a 12-step program, Edward was systematically working through a list to avoid slipping back into his old ways. He needed to forgive others and himself. He needed to apologize for the ways he had hurt some people in his life. Back in his room, he opened the drawer and examined the contents. Edward picked up the wooden elephant.

It had been nearly five years since he had traveled back to Ohio to visit his family. Before that, it had been eleven years. He had no plans to go back again. Five years ago, he had traveled home to preside over his mother's funeral, but two years later, he had turned down the opportunity to be the celebrant for his father's. He thought back over his reasoning.

It had been easy to forgive his mother. She had simply been obedient to the life that was passed down to her. The daughter of wealth and faith, she had dutifully produced children to give back to the Lord—some for family life and some for the religious life. She had buried one son, George, taken by God before the world could take his purity. Edward's mother had slowly faded after that, but no one could blame her. She had fulfilled her calling already and had given her husband a full life—it wasn't her fault that he hadn't risen to the occasion.

Edward's father had only stepped up to the occasion in the early years of the marriage. It was easy to see in the old family photographs. His father, with his striking good looks, looked pleased with his expensive suit and commanding presence. One set of pictures had been taken with the entire family when Edward was just a baby. Only the rich could afford such pictures, and his family had many of them. That year, they posed for a Christmas photo, and Edward was only a month old. His mother looked tired, not from his birth but most likely from the lingering grief of losing George only months before. His father, who never smiled, had pride in his eyes. The men had surely been drinking before the pictures and had bolstered that pride, just for show. In reality, Edward's father had already resigned himself to a nondescript life. But the days, months, and years following George's death were the precise timeframe in which they did not need his father's resignation. These were the moments his father should have emerged as a strong, yet loving leader for his mother and their family. In real life, not just in the pictures. But, from then on, Edward's father withdrew until he faded into the background completely. Or, had he withdrawn even before George's death?

Edward wondered, why had it taken his father's boat so long to get to the family pier at Silver Lake on George's tragic day? For so long, Edward had figured his mother's morning sickness, from her pregnancy with Edward, had delayed his father. But maybe there was more to that. Had he stopped somewhere on that morning drive? Had he seen someone? Or had he just stopped to stare across one of the other lakes, like Edward would see him do many times? Was he simply delaying retrieving his active son and seeing his intimidating in-laws? No matter the reason, the outcome would never change. While Edward's father delayed, George had slipped unseen into the dark, unyielding water below.

Edward did forgive his father, of course, but he just couldn't summon the energy to return to his hometown and to his father's funeral. The bulk of his family had been mocking Edward's desire to go west for years, and they whispered that he must be hiding something. Nothing would change his close relationship with his sisters in the religious life, especially Eleanor. Still, the others didn't understand him, and they were happy to have another reason to write him off. They had other family priests nearby who had stayed loyal to their Ohio roots. They hadn't run off to the west, like Edward, like some sort of cowboy preacher.

When Edward first went to seminary in Chicago with the intention of settling in the west, those critical family members began their gossip. What is he running from? They all asked. What is he hiding? Only his mother, Eleanor, and, of course, cousin Gigi, later with the Sisters of the Precious Blood, understood that Edward had a missionary mindset. The West needed more Roman Catholics, and Edward answered the call.

When their grandfather, Grosspapa, died, Edward was summoned from the seminary to return for the funeral and the reading of the will. He hadn't been particularly close to his grandfather, who was naturally too busy to form strong attachments to his grandchildren. An orphan from a very young age, Luke had never learned family affection. He had been apprenticed at fifteen in carpentry, and that became his sole focus and vocation. Through it all—immigration, marriage, and raising ten children—Luke kept his focus on building and then later on his building supply company. His children and grandchildren had all been taught to revere him and to live up to his expectations of raising Catholic families or entering the religious life. Their grandmother adored her husband, and all her grandchildren adored her, so they did their best to show Grosspapa the affection due. It was no secret that the family had a lot of money, and everyone had their ideas about what would happen to it.

It had been fun for Edward to see Gigi again at the funeral and the reception afterward. Gigi followed Edward outside and told him she would have a cigarette for old times' sake. "We aren't allowed to smoke at the Precious Blood Convent. You are allowed at St. Joseph's?"

"It is Chicago, after all, and maybe that's why I chose it." Edward laughed. "I'm curious why you chose to be with the Sisters of the Precious Blood. Don't tell me that you just liked the name?"

"I heard the cry of the blood, of course," Gigi raised her eyebrows at him. "Then I answered the call. That's what we are told anyway, and I do like the sound of it. I really did feel called into missionary work. I hope to move to their convent in Guatemala and help with their missionary work there. Did you go see Eleanor up north? I envy her contentment in her call to a life of prayer. It does comfort me to know she is praying, especially for us, her religious relatives."

"Yes, I drove up on Thursday. Grossmama insisted I take two of the little girl cousins with me so, as she put it, 'they could see if they hear the call of the blessed, religious life.' It just felt awkward to me, and I'm sure it was even more so for them. They had to sit in the back seat for two hours each way with a complete stranger as their driver. I just smoked more than usual and let them try out the electric windows. I did take them for ice cream on the way back. It was great to see Eleanor, of course. Always an angel."

"Yes, she is." Gigi agreed. "Always one of Grosspapa's favorites. Wasn't she summoned as well, for the reading of the will?"

"Yes, but there was a provision for her, since that would mean breaking her prayer rule. What do you think is going to happen at the reading?"

Gigi rolled her eyes, just like the old days. "Well, we can assume that most of his money will go to St. Benedict's and then to his favorite seminary. Perhaps some will go to your seminary and to my convent? I can't imagine why we were summoned otherwise. The rest of the money will surely be for Grossmama's care and then also go to our parents."

"Then our parents will just recycle it back into the church, and the same old story will continue," Edward added.

"Edward?" His mother stuck her head out from the side door. "I think everyone has left except those who are staying for the reading. Would you and Eugenia please join us?"

The reading was quite different from what they imagined. Their family was huge, so it was a huge gathering, and there was tension in the room that hadn't been there at the funeral. Edward's uncles and cousins, who had become priests before him, had a look of superiority. These were the ones who had stayed local, after all, and were the family's favorites. They were all dressed well, and Edward quickly brushed off the front of his faded, hand-me-down cassock.

The attorney got right down to business and read a letter written by Luke. It was short and to the point until it reached the end. In essence, it said that all his own children had lived up to their vocations in work and ministry and didn't need any financial help. He was very proud of their work ethic and stewardship. He had helped each of them in turn with college and seminary, and none of them had suffered for any want. One son, Edward's Uncle Stephen, would continue running the business supply company, and those details had already been settled. Of course, Grossmama would always be cared for.

Therefore, in addition to the church and his chosen seminary and convent, a designated portion of the inheritance would go to the grandchildren. Depending on their situation, there was enough for each of them to purchase property or to finish college or seminary. This was when the letter became a little more personal than usual for their grandfather.

The attorney read, "I am adding two things that may come as a surprise to you, but this reflects something that I have regretted in my life. At this age, I have come to regret not having passed on the virtue of humility to my children and grandchildren. Our family has been blessed financially, and perhaps I have allowed pride and indulgence to reign. Please forgive me. These are not traits that I would want passed on. Sadly, it may be too late for some of you. I hope you will all take time to study the scriptures on what it means to live a life of humility. Two of my grandchildren have shown humility—perhaps they received it as a gift from the Lord, or maybe their mother taught them. She has been a beautiful example to me. I want to entrust a larger portion of my inheritance to them, as I am confident they will distribute the wealth with godly wisdom. Therefore, I am dividing the rest of my money between two of my grandchildren, Eleanor and Edward."

It was as if the room went cold, and you could hear a pin drop. Edward immediately looked at his parents. His mother had tears in her eyes and a look of complete serenity, as if nothing in the world could have made her happier than hearing that two of her children had shown humility. Grosspapa had been referring to her, then, as one who taught her children well. Edward's father was unreadable, as usual, but now he even looked more like a statue than normal. Had he married his wife for money? Maybe his whole adult life and his original intentions had led to this singular moment, and now what?

Edward looked at Gigi next. There wasn't an ounce of bitterness in her. It was like she was cheering him on, as she always had.

But what did it really matter? What would Edward do with this money? The pressure was already beginning to suffocate him, along with the looks of bitterness from everyone else in the room. Edward couldn't get out of there fast enough and back to St. Joe's.

Edward was too busy to deal much with the money in the years that followed. He made occasional donations to his seminary and Pacific Garden Mission, for example, but it was as if the Lord was immediately putting any so-called virtue to the test. Eleanor had probably handled her money immediately, in her usual angelic way—with a message directly from God Himself.

Most of the family had snubbed Edward due to the inheritance. But he had braved the judge and jury to go home for his grandmother's and then his mother's funeral. By the time his father had passed away, everyone had surely heard about Edward's transgression, and, save Gigi and Eleanor, the family was finished with him completely. Even the thought of standing before his father's coffin made Edward feel small. But Edward did not harbor any bitterness toward his father or any of his family. He was finally free of them.

That brought Edward's thoughts back to the question about whom he needed to forgive. He dropped the elephant and picked up the obsidian arrowhead. He is not sure why he has kept it this long. Perhaps to punish himself? The very nature of an arrowhead symbolized death and darkness. Of course, it didn't start out representing those things for Edward back when he was a young priest at his first post in Delta City.

It had become at least a weekly event for Edward to dine with Francis and the Murphy family. The whole family was enchanted by Edward, and they enchanted him. Francis's father, Murph, like his wife, Teresa, and Francis, had a great sense of humor. He claimed to be 100% Irish, and drinking and joking were his favorite pastimes. He was wickedly smart, as they all liked to say. He worked as a water master, but this wasn't satisfactory to him. His real dream was to invent toys and games, but, of course, that wasn't practical for feeding his newly expanded family of five. Anthony had been born, and Murph and Teresa had given him the middle name Edward— after their new friend.

Edward saw glimpses of Murph's job dissatisfaction in his temper, but he mostly controlled himself around mixed company. Edward knew that Teresa and the boys felt safe when he was around, so they wanted him around as much as possible. Murph didn't mind. He loved to tease Edward for his Eastern ways and lack of life experience.

"We know what happened, Father Edward! You couldn't find a fun, pretty girl back in Ohio, so you threw your hat in for the priesthood." Murph laughed at his own joke, "You came to the West and realized too late that all the pretty girls were here in California. Sorry about your luck!"

Teresa would always laugh heartily at all the jokes, and that surprised Edward at first. The women back home were more reserved. Murph was right about the pretty women in the West, and Teresa was the most fun and the loveliest woman he had ever met. He was captivated by her ready laugh and smile. Always a bit shy himself, Teresa had taken to laughing at Edward's expense—especially when the adults sat around late in the evening smoking. The women in his family, save Gigi's occasional cigarette, did not smoke or drink, so this part of Teresa intrigued him as well.

"Is that true, Father Edward? You became a priest because you couldn't find a girl?" Teresa asked during one of those late evenings when Francis, Joseph, and Anthony had already gone to bed. "Tell us all. You know what they say, 'many a slip be twixt the cup and the lip.'" She winked at him.

Edward felt slow when he tried to match Murph and Teresa's wit, and it always took him a moment to collect his thoughts. "No, no, of course that wasn't the reason. I just, uh, always knew I would be a priest. I never looked for a girlfriend." Edward could recall many girls teasing him for the same reasons Teresa did. Gigi had told Edward that they teased him because they liked him. This thought disturbed him, and he began to wonder if Teresa liked him in that way.

"Oh, you never looked for a girlfriend? Sure!" Teresa replied with her usual spunk. Then she started singing mischievously—"Caviar comes from virgin sturgeon, virgin sturgeon's a very fine fish. Virgin sturgeon needs no urgin', that's why caviar is my dish. I fed my caviar to my…"

Murph held up his hand to Teresa, "That's probably too much for the father, Teresa." And then to Edward he said, "You will have to excuse my wife—she loves fishing."

Edward couldn't even think of a response as he tried to process the words of her song.

Most of those evenings were full of Teresa's stories. She was a true Westerner, having grown up on a Wyoming ranch by a river. They had chickens and cattle, and eventually, after moving to a 100-acre farm in Idaho, they grew potatoes and onions. When the rivers froze in the winter, Teresa and her siblings would ice skate on them. Teresa told them of the year they had dairy cows, and each child had their own cow to milk twice a day.

"My cow loved the warmth of the manure pile and would lie on it," Teresa told them, laughing. "So that meant she was covered in manure every time I went to milk her. She was the only one who did that. I'm sure I went to school each day smelling like manure. The upshot of it was that the dairy cows lasted only a year before my dad sold them. The next thing was the Bermuda onions, and he would pay us 15 cents a row to weed them. He would be watching to see if we were sloppy in our weeding. If I pulled an onion out, I would try to replant it—he always caught me, of course. At harvest time, he would pay us by the bag. But one year, the market was flooded with onions, and they weren't worth anything. I remember he took all the bags and dumped the onions out in Rock Creek Canyon. You see, the bags were worth more than the onions. So that year, we kids didn't make anything from all that picking. So after that, Father got into hogs, and he let each one of us have one. They were our responsibility to feed. We grew alfalfa, too, and I took my job very seriously. Every day, I would bring in a big armload of alfalfa for my hog. I was determined he would be the fattest. My siblings and I were always in competition with each other, you see. And I was the feistiest of all of us."

Edward could believe it. Teresa was nothing like the girls back home. Gigi was the feistiest in their family—that was true, but none of the women did outdoor labor or enjoyed outdoor adventures. The only outdoor activity the men did was fishing, and the women never went along. Edward was fascinated to meet a true Western woman with endless stories.

He could tell Murph enjoyed all of his wife's stories, too. He chimed in one evening by saying, "You can't take the outdoors out of Teresa. I saw her really brighten up recently when we began to go up to the Cedarville area for my work. I think it reminds Teresa of her early years in Wyoming. Some of the last Indian wars took place up near Cedarville, and there is a lot of evidence still from the Indians' lives there."

"Oh, yes!" Teresa agreed. "The boys and I have found countless arrowheads there on our hikes while Murph checks the water."

Edward couldn't even imagine. He had only been hiking once in his life, and that was with Billy Sunday back in the Chicago area. They had driven quite a distance to get to Starved Rock, but it had been worth it. It was the most rugged place Edward had ever seen. Ohio was so flat in comparison. Billy Sunday had talked about the worldwide flood creating the dramatic landscape. Ohio had only been left with flat land and countless lakes. Teresa interrupted his thoughts by tapping him on his shoulder. She said, "Here. You can have this one. But, mum's the word—we aren't supposed to carry them away."

Edward was slow to react as Teresa let her hand linger on his shoulder. Then she reached around and picked up Edward's hand in hers and opened his fingers. She placed an arrowhead on his palm and then closed his fingers around it.

Edward just remembers feeling ashamed at how he felt in that moment. He tried to shake the feeling by examining the arrowhead, but it was tough. This was all wrong, he thought. But that was the most female contact he had had in recent memory, and he couldn't get it out of his mind. The only thing that would help was to hold the arrowhead tight enough that the sharp edges would dig into his palm.

When he left the Murphy house that evening, he knew he should walk fast and never look back. He should throw the arrowhead into the bushes lining their yard and be done with them all. But, instead, he clasped it tighter and, only later, would he know the irreparable damage that came from not letting go.

Chapter 18

Christine visited Dochero alone one last time during her time as a holdover at Mt. St. Paul's. The late-spring temperatures in Pine Valley were perfect for long walks, and she left early in the morning to give herself plenty of time to wander and pray. Sister Mary Rita had been keeping her busy with religious readings, and Christine had found a small quote from St. Teresa of Avila that she enjoyed repeating to herself— "For prayer is nothing else than being on terms of friendship with God."

Christine loved that thought, and in fact, it was something she had always felt—friendship with God. It was as natural to her as breathing. That was the feeling she felt when she thought back to her golden bedroom at home with the tidy little beds, windows, and lamps. It was so comforting to lie there in the quiet, hearing the voices outside her room. It was contentment and peace she felt then, like God was near and it was ok just to simply exist with Him. That peace was more challenging to feel when it was her mother and Patrick fighting on the other side of her walls, however, and this was what she wanted to talk to God about on her walk to Dochero.

She still didn't have any answers for why she hadn't been picked up from school yet, and it was embarrassing to think that her family hadn't paid her school bills. It made Christine feel like she was an orphan. It was the first time in her life that she wasn't surrounded by family or friends. At first, she had been sleeping in the large dormitory by herself, but then Sister Mary Rita moved her to one of the old nuns' bedrooms on the third floor so repairs could be done in the dormitory.

Sister Mary Rita tried to comfort her, "Don't worry, Dear. I wrote to your mother and told her the same thing, 'Don't worry.' In fact, I told her that we had even considered asking your mother to let you stay behind anyway. It is quite providential how it all worked out. I told your mother to pray to the Holy Infant of Prague concerning her financial concerns. He will surely help her. Do you know of this statue of the infant Jesus? There have been miraculous healings attributed to the Holy Infant, and in 1639, when Prague was saved during the Swedish siege, they attributed it to the Holy Infant." Sister Mary Rita crossed herself then.

This gave Christine a lot to think about, and for the first few days, she pretended to be a nun with that room as her cell. The feeling there was much like it was in her home bedroom. It was very sweet and simple in there, and she loved the time of kneeling and praying by her little bed. She had a long list that she would go through each time she said her prayers. She asked the Holy Infant of Prague to join her in her prayers.

"Please, Lord, bring grace, mercy, peace, and healing to my mother, Francis, Joseph, Anthony, Samuel, Patrick, Jr., Abigail, Maggie, Phyllis, and Nancy. Please remember our President, Georgia, and Tank—I mean, Julie—in your kingdom. Please be with Putt Putt, my father, Murph, wherever he is, and even be with Patrick."

It was hard for Christine to pray for her father and Patrick. They were both strangers to her. This was the one area where Christine indulged in self-pity. She knew it was wrong to feel sorry for herself, but she would allow herself to go there now and then. On her walk to Dochero that morning, she had spiraled in her thinking, and now her gait was more like a shuffle.

"What is it going to be like when I finally get to go home?" she wondered. "Maybe Patrick won't even live there anymore, or maybe I will have to go testify against him in court. What would I even say? That he had never loved me? I was just an innocent little girl when he first came into our life—who couldn't love a little girl?" Christine began to cry. She had seen happy families in church—fathers doting on their children, especially their precious little girls. Her own father had abandoned her before she was even born, and then her stepfather never accepted her during the most vulnerable time of a child's life.

It seemed that Christine was to go through life fatherless. She straightened herself up and took a big breath. "Get over yourself," she thought. "Lord, have mercy on me, a sinner," she prayed. Nancy didn't have a dad either, and that was true for many people she knew. There was no point in feeling sorry for herself. If Patrick left, they would all have to deal with it. As Christine quickened her pace and swung her arms vigorously to try to snap out of her sorrow, she thought of a newspaper clipping her mom had sent in one of the last letters. The clipping featured a photo of Teresa with a walking stick and the headline "In memory of JFK, Teresa Harrison has taken up the JFK Challenge to Walk 50 Miles in Under 20 Hours!"

Mom had actually done it! She had walked from Lakeview to Alturas in less than 20 hours. The letter said that Patrick had driven beside her with food, coffee, and water. "That was gallant of him," Christine thought. Her mom was truly a marvel. Christine had never met a more beautiful or energetic mom among all of her friends' moms. I guess her mom more than made up for the lack of a father, and Christine decided to be thankful. Christine stood taller and sucked in her stomach, thinking of Teresa.

When she arrived at Dochero, the morning mist still clung to the little ravine, and it was cold. Christine made her way down to sit beside the stream, and it felt warmer down there. Christine decided to pray and offer gratitude for the family she did have.

"Dear God, I am sorry for my self-indulgent thoughts about not having a dad. Forgive me if I get sad once in a while, but I will try just to be thankful for my mom and my siblings. They are all so wonderful. And there is no one like our mother in the whole world. Remember the life-sized nativities she would haul up onto the roof with Francis? I can hear their laughter and excitement even now. I know she is competitive and vain, but at least she was determined to show everyone how important the birth of your Son was for our family. Her sins are many, but I saw the way she prayed to you on her knees. I just love her so much, and I am not sure I have told her. Please give me a chance to tell her."

Christine's heart felt like it wanted to burst with love for her mom, and a long-ago memory came to mind, another time when she had felt so close to her.

It must have been when they first moved into their new home, with Patrick, and Christine felt the sting of his rejection. That particular night, a dramatic thunderstorm had woken Christine and, in that big house, it felt like her mom was miles away. Christine cried out a few times before climbing out of bed to search for Teresa. As she approached the closed door of her mother's bedroom, she heard Patrick say, "Just leave her be, she needs to toughen up."

Just after that, the door opened and Teresa came out wearing a beautiful satin robe that Christine had never seen. The smell of Estée Lauder that followed her mother immediately clouded out Christine's fears.

"This is quite a storm, isn't it, Chrissy? The lightning must be very close. I know just what to do. Come with me."

Teresa took Chrissy's hand and led her to the corner of the living room, where she had placed some palm leaves from church in a basket. "I learned this from stories about my great-grandmother—she was a clairvoyant, they say. Some people at the church might not approve, but I like to burn palm leaves to ask for God's protection against a fierce storm. Here, let's go burn these out by the front door."

Chrissy followed Teresa and reached out to lightly hold the end of her mom's bathrobe tie. It felt so cool and silky.

Lightning lit up the sky just as Teresa opened the door, and an immediate clap of thunder shook the ground underneath Chrissy's feet. Chrissy grabbed around Teresa's waist.

"It's ok, Chrissy. God will protect us. Just wait."

Teresa squatted down near the front door out of the rain and wind and placed the palm leaves in the depression of a large rock that had once been used by the Indians to grind grain. She lit the palm leaves on fire with matches and then prayed out loud,

"Protect, we ask you, O Lord, this house against the assaults of our spiritual enemies, and cause the present dreadful disorder of the air to cease. We offer you, O Lord, our praises and sacrifices in thanksgiving for the favors we have already received. Lord, please hear our humble prayers, that we may rejoice in the ceasing of this storm, and always make a good use of the grant of your favors. Amen."

They crossed themselves, stood in silence for a moment, and watched the smoldering leaves before Teresa softly closed the door and led Chrissy back to her room.

After Teresa tucked her in, Christine said, "Thank you."

In her heart, she yearned for Teresa to climb into bed with her, but that hadn't happened since they moved in with Patrick. They used to all sleep in one room at the French Hotel during the winter, or in one tent when they camped in the summer. At first, her mother had kept a crib for Christine in the tent. Teresa told everyone, "We need to keep her off the floor so the rattlesnakes don't gobble her up." Later, she had let Christine sleep with her in the bed, with the three chickens roosting at their feet at night. "Each of you got a chick in your Easter basket, but only three lived long enough to go to Modoc with us for the summer. They free ranged around camp all day and roosted at our feet at night. It was me, five kids, and three chickens in one tent," Teresa recalled with pride.

Christine had always felt so cozy being all together—before Patrick. She watched her mom walk away that stormy night, but after their conversation, she trusted that she would be ok. Somehow, she sensed a comforting presence in her new golden bedroom. Through heavy eyelids, Christine saw her mom kiss her fingers and then touch the crucifix on the wall—then Teresa suddenly turned back.

"You know what, Chrissy, I think I want to stay close to you until we know that God has taken the storm away."

Teresa crawled into Christine's bed, and Christine snuggled in close, relishing the feel of the satin robe, the smell of the perfume, and her mother all to herself.

"Would you please tell me more about the great-grandmother who used to burn palm leaves?"

"Yes, of course, but we must whisper. We don't want anyone to find us." Teresa squeezed Christine as she laughed softly. "It would be your great-great-grandmother, Mary Margaret. My mother, Theodora, may she have eternal rest, was Mary Margaret's granddaughter."

"I love both of their names," Christine whispered, feeling so safe and snug.

"It was Mary Margaret's grandmother who was from French royalty, but she left her family to marry their gardener. They moved to the United States, and it is said that she never regretted leaving her royal family to take an adventure to America. Do you know what that means?" Teresa whispered.

"What?" Christine asked.

"It means that you come from French royalty, too!"

"Wow!" Christine whispered back, even as her eyelids grew heavier.

"Well, Mary Margaret was called a clairvoyant, and she is the one who used to burn palm leaves to keep away danger. My mother told me that one day a blackbird landed on Mary Margaret's shoulder while she worked in the garden, and it pecked her cheek before falling down dead. Mary Margaret said, 'I am going to die.' And she did. Not there in the garden, mind you, but during that night."

Christine, nearly asleep, thought that the bird sounded a little scary, but she just hugged her mom tighter and softly whispered, "Thank you, Mary Margaret, for helping mom scare away the thunderstorm."

"That was God and our Blessed Mother, Chrissy. But I sure do like to think about my great-grandmother, Mary Margaret. You were my miracle child, and sometimes I wonder if you might be like Mary Margaret. That's all she wrote, for now. Sleep well, my sweet girl."

Christine brought herself back to the present, but it was as if she could still feel her mother's arms around her and feel that satin bathrobe. That time with her mother and learning about Mary Margaret were the reasons Christine chose the name Margaret for her confirmation name. It was one of her most treasured memories with her mother.

"God, please forgive me for not telling her how much I love her. Please, God, make sure that my mom is ok and that I will see her again soon. Help me to appreciate her more, rather than think of my lack of a father."

As tears fell from her eyes and she sat in silence, Christine heard a soft but clear voice.

"I am collecting your tears in a bottle—they are precious to me. A broken and contrite heart is a beautiful thing. It's ok if you are sad sometimes. Don't change that. Nor your heart of gratitude. It is beautiful. Nurture that in your life, too. Thankfulness forms the soul. When you see the broken things in the world, just remember that your real home is in heaven. Before too long, we will be there together. Don't lose heart. I love you."

It felt like Christine had been holding her breath, and when the voice stopped, she exhaled loudly and doubled over on the stream bank.

Had God just spoken to her? As a father would? Sister Mary Rita said that God only speaks to His children when it is silent. And what about those words about the broken things in the world? That sounded vaguely familiar.

Christine's breath came steady now, and she felt completely serene inside. She felt so warm, too. God was indeed her real father, and He loved her. She had heard it all so clearly and audibly, so it had to be true.

"Please, God, I never want to forget this moment as long as I live. Thank you. Thank you for this place—Dochero. I am not sure I will ever visit here again after today, even though I promised Nancy. Nothing could ever be as special as what just happened. Thank you, God. I love you, too."

Chapter 19

Saturday morning, Edward opened the back door to find Margaret's family crowded on the landing waiting for him.

"Ready, Father?" Matthew asked in such a commanding tone that Edward knew it was not actually a question. Matthew was holding Andrew in his brace, and Andrew, Anne, and Margaret were all looking at Edward expectantly.

"Of course, and good morning, I have been looking forward to it," Edward answered. "Why don't we let Margaret lead the way?"

"Sure!" Margaret piped up, like a songbird. "I can't wait to show you our 'Dochero!'"

"It's stuff and nonsense, I'm sure," Matthew said gruffly.

"Matthew, please, we need to believe for Andrew's sake." Anne placed her hand on Matthew's arm and looked at him endearingly.

Edward felt his heart flood with love for this family, and he had to put aside his memory of the Murphy family from long ago. "Please, God, let today be about this family, not the other. Lord Jesus Christ, have mercy on me, a sinner." Edward kept repeating this phrase in prayer so that his mind wouldn't wander.

Edward followed along after the family this way for a while before speaking up, "Matthew, may I help carry Andrew for a spell?"

Matthew looked back in surprise, and Edward saw Anne nod slightly to Matthew.

"I guess you may, but I doubt you will be able to for long. Andrew is quite heavy, and I don't imagine you do much heavy lifting?"

"Father Edward is strong from all of his prostrations, aren't you?" Margaret interrupted.

Edward wondered how she knew about his prostrations, but he just answered weakly, "Oh no, not many."

"Matthew, please let Father try." Again, Anne put her hand on Matthew's arm.

Edward reached out, and Matthew showed him where best to hold onto the cumbersome brace.

"Well, hello, Andrew. How are you today?" Edward asked as they commenced walking.

Andrew just stared intently at Edward, so Edward kept talking.

"It has been a while since I have gotten to hold such a fine chap as yourself. I bet you are excited to go down to the creek and to cross the bridge?"

Andrew gave a little nod, and Edward continued. "It will be fun to see the big Pelton wheel. Have you seen it before?"

Andrew shook his head.

"Well, the Pelton wheel took advantage of the rushing water during the gold mining days. This one is the largest in the world! They used it for around thirty years. Water contains so much power, and the men harnessed that energy."

"Do you think the water's power will heal me?" Andrew asked softly.

Edward was taken aback at the quiet voice and at Andrew's question.

How could he answer Andrew without giving him too much hope?

"We can ask God to heal you in those waters, but then we also have to ask God to help us accept whatever His will might be."

Andrew nodded with a look of wisdom in his eyes. "Yes, I know. God has His best for me. I know that. Even if He doesn't heal me, it's just my father that I am worried about. He doesn't have that same trust in God. If God doesn't heal me, my father might just be angry at Him."

Already nervous about the whole morning, Edward grew more anxious. He prayed silently for a while longer before answering Andrew. "You sure are a wise and brave little boy. We can only pray and ask God to heal your father's heart, despite what happens in the water. I like praying the way people in the Bible prayed when they wanted to be healed. Would you like to try?"

Andrew nodded.

Edward said, "Let's pray like this. Lord Jesus Christ, have mercy on me, a sinner."

Andrew repeated Edward and then said, "I heard you talk about that at church."

Edward looked into those deep eyes again and answered, "Of course you did, you are an attentive and perceptive child. You are a precious lamb of God."

Andrew was starting to get heavy, but Edward was determined to carry him all the way. He could see the Pelton wheel at the top of the hill. "Look, Andrew, there is the wheel!"

Anne came back to stand next to Andrew then. "Do you see it, Darling? That is a very famous piece of mining equipment there. They found more gold in Pine Valley during the gold rush than in any other California town. Even when Pine Valley burned, they quickly rebuilt and kept the mine going. Your great-grandfather was part of the gold rush and did very well."

"How come we aren't rich, then?" Margaret demanded.

"Because he was foolish with his money, that's why," Matthew answered.

"That is true," Anne agreed. "He was greedy and impulsive and not a good steward of his earnings. He lived a life of sin, truth be told."

"That is unfortunate for us, I guess," Margaret said with a sigh. "But this Dochero is a special place. Maybe the same blessing that made the water rich in gold will make it healing for Andrew."

"It better be something. Something more than just freezing cold for Andrew." Matthew said in frustration.

"It's ok, Dad, I'm not scared of the cold," Andrew spoke up. "Father Edward? Is it ok for me to be baptized this way?"

"It isn't the usual way these days, but we did it this way in Chicago occasionally with the Pacific Garden Mission. I will put you under the water three times to represent the Father, the Son, and the Holy Spirit. Will you be ok with that?"

Andrew nodded.

"Also, when we get down there, I want to hear in your own words why you are choosing to be baptized."

Andrew nodded solemnly again.

As they crossed the bridge, Anne stopped midway and looked down at the water. "Yes, this was Christine's place. She called it Dochero, too. Did you know her, Father? She attended Mt. St. Paul's in the '60s?"

Edward answered quickly, "I wasn't here in the '60s, so no, I did not." Meeting someone a few times didn't count as knowing them, Edward tried to reassure himself.

"Did you know her well?" Edward turned the question back to Anne.

"I was older than her, but we crossed paths a few times. Mostly, I saw her from a distance. Our family was poor, and I envied the girls who got to attend Mt. St. Paul's. I would watch from a spot in the trees from across the street when the boarders first pulled up with their parents. After a while, it was easy to see that everyone was putting on airs that first day. Many families were troubled and hoped the school would somehow save their daughters. You could tell the troubled girls right away. Even though their parents, or parent, walked with their heads held high, dressed in their finest, carrying the tidy suitcases, and wearing their best smile, the troubled daughter was downcast and sullen. They knew the whole plan was doomed before it even started. But Christine was different. All she showed was joy and peace, like this was heaven itself. Her mother was definitely putting on a show—she was quite pretty and spunky, and very fashionable. But the difference was

Christine was all hope and sweetness and not fazed by whatever her mother was doing."

Edward was surprised by his emotion and quickly held Andrew against him with one arm so that he could catch a tear behind his glasses. He pushed his glasses up and wiped his nose. He felt Andrew watching him.

Anne kept talking, and Andrew was growing very heavy. "I was jealous of Christine for all of those reasons. She had a fashionable, vivacious mother—my mother was always so mousy and depressed, and I also envied the air of complete joy that seemed to surround Christine everywhere she went— like a beam of sunshine. Something was definitely different about her."

Edward sniffed and interrupted, "Well, should we get down there and see why good old Andrew wants to get baptized?"

"Well, that's exactly what I wanted to say," Anne answered emphatically. "I came down here one day and found Christine. It was really misty that morning, and it was easy for me to hide from her. It's like she was talking to herself or praying. Even with all that mist, I am not kidding when I say that her face was shining like the sun. And then it was so strange, she went into the water as if she was baptizing herself."

That's when Edward's knees felt like they were going to buckle. He pushed Andrew toward Matthew and grabbed the bridge railing.

Now all eyes were on him.

Anne added one last thing, "It is a little awkward to say, but she did it naked."

Chapter 20

Christine was gathering her thoughts that morning at Dochero and preparing to say goodbye to the spot forever. She pondered the memory of the thunderstorm and what her mother said about her great-grandmother, Mary Margaret. Then, Teresa also called Christine a miracle child.

What did she mean by that? Perhaps it was because her parents were divorced by the time she was born? Or because she was the first girl after four boys. She was the only child out of all eight who was born in the winter, too.

It's no wonder that her mother spoiled her so much. It sometimes made her feel sick—so much attention.

If she were a miracle child, did that mean she was clairvoyant, as her mother had suggested a time or two? Sister Mary Rita had warned them multiple times about entertaining such thoughts.

"Things of that nature can be straight from the devil disguised as light. Reject every vision or thought immediately as if it were straight from hell itself. Take every thought captive."

This made Christine feel nervous about those words she thought had come from God. "God, please, protect me from the evil one. I only want to hear from you."

Christine sat down and felt like crying. Just a moment ago, she was so elated, but now she already felt downtrodden again. Is everyone this way or just me? Maybe I am just sensitive or weird. Everyone else is marching along and not noticing much.

It was a smell then, faint, but sweet, that broke Christine's reverie.

The smell was not overly sweet, more like jasmine in the breeze.

"That's the scent of water," Christine said out loud. "Mother taught us about the scent of water all those years ago when we camped at Deep Creek. She used to say this, I think it was a quote from the Bible, 'Yet, at the scent of water it will bud and put forth shoots like a plant.'"

Christine let the memories come, and she took in the scent. Some of the memories were most likely formed from family pictures or from hearing her brothers' stories, but either way, they were so vivid to her.

They had used a big wall tent for their home at Deep Creek, with an old cookstove sitting outside. Somehow, her mother had gotten her friends' husbands to bring an actual bed frame and mattress up for her, and their chickens roosted on her footboard at night. Christine got to sleep in the bed with her mother, then, while her brothers were pleased as punch to sleep in cowboy bedrolls.

Christine had only been eighteen months old when they camped all summer for the first time. Her mother was so wise. She would rent out their house in Delta City for the four months they camped and was able to save up quite a bit of money that way. The Delta City Bee published a front-page article about the "model mother" who camped alone with her five children. The picture showed Teresa loading up the kids and all the gear to head to the mountains where "rattlesnakes and mountain lions abound."

Christine didn't think it was possible to have a happier childhood when she recalled those times. There was no father in the picture, but her older brothers more than made up for it. Along with the sounds of the creek, the rustling leaves, crickets, and songbirds, the near-constant laughter meant they were surrounded by pure joy. Christine took up whistling at a young age since everyone in the family whistled throughout the day.

They were living like wild children, and they all were as happy as could be. The kids would climb young fir trees and sway back and forth near the top—pretending they were riding horses. Their mom would hunt early in the mornings, sometimes taking Christine along in a pack. There may have been nothing that Teresa enjoyed more than hiking and hunting in the early mornings. She especially liked to sneak off by herself while the others slept.

They ate fish often—freshly caught from the stream by the boys, with the hellgrammites Teresa found there for bait. The boys had been ecstatic when Joseph was able to shoot the rattlesnake that Teresa had found inside a cardboard suitcase in their tent—they had eaten that, too. Teresa rounded out their diet with salads made from the fresh watercress she collected from the streambed. She also showed them how to rub the watercress on their faces to remove blemishes and freckles.

Teresa had given them more freedom than most children, living outside as they did. But there had been one strict warning all of the time—"It is fine to climb trees, but always climb back down. Do not jump from the heights. That is how J.B. died."

They had all heard the story several times, at least one time by the fire out at Deep Creek. Their mother's voice was low and foreboding then. "J.B. was a redhead, like you, Francis. My parents were sure happy that you were born a redhead, like their son in Heaven. His real name was Joseph, named after my father—your namesake, too, Joseph. J.B. usually got into a fair amount of trouble, the little rascal. I would usually tattle on him. Maybe I liked being the only troublemaker and didn't want to share that title with him. I think I was always trying to get my mother's attention by getting in trouble or tattling. One time, J.B. had gotten into the carbolic acid kept out in the barn. I think they used it to treat animal wounds and parasites. Well, anyway, one day I found J.B. hiding in the corner, and he had burns on him from getting into the acid. Of course, I tattled on him since we had been strictly forbidden to touch it. It wasn't too long later that he died, and I could always picture him with those burns. I felt bad for tattling and knew I was somehow responsible for his death."

"Is that how he died, from the acid?" Samuel asked.

"No, but it wasn't too long later. Remember, we had to get rid of the ranch and our nice house in town when my father got caught by the revenuers for his bootlegging. Remember, even the sheriff, Frank Toy, was in cahoots with him."

"Oh, yeah!" Samuel piped up. Of course, all the boys loved this story.

"J.B. was eleven when that happened, and I was only seven. The older kids weren't with us at the time. Good thing, too, since we had to pack all our possessions into one car and still fit five of us kids in. Oh, my mother was low then. She hadn't been happy about my father and his shenanigans, but then to lose everything and have to flee in the dead of night. She really married down by marrying him. Her family had owned a huge flour mill in Ohio, after all. Remember, my dad's first job was as a gravedigger."

All the kids let out an exclamation then.

"My poor mother, things only got worse. Much worse. Dad left her and all of us kids on his brother's farm, and J.B. was left up to himself. Dad had to go back and settle things with the revenuers. I guess he must have paid them off with all the money from the land and house. So we were on the farm, and our uncle kept an old hackney in the barn, like a carriage. We loved playing in it, and the adults never watched us. J.B. had Paul and me sit inside while he acted like the carriage driver.

While he was playing around, he decided to climb up on top and then jump down to scare away the thievin' highwaymen. I remember watching him jump off in front of our window, and I couldn't wait to tattle on him. But there was no need—he had misjudged the distance, and it was a harder landing than he had imagined. His appendix burst on impact, and there was nothing anyone could do. Our father got back in time from his dealings to see him before he died. They called Marion back from school, where she was on scholarship. She didn't make it back in time to see him, but she still lost her scholarship and never went back. That was a shame. It was a very dark time, and I felt responsible somehow.

"It couldn't have been your fault, Mom," Francis spoke up across the fire from Teresa.

"Oh, I don't know. Sins affect the whole world, not just ourselves. I think I have always harbored some resentment toward my father. It was obvious that his sins led to J.B.'s death. The bootlegging was the only reason we were on that farm in the first place."

"Wasn't he just trying to provide for his family?" Anthony asked.

"Bootlegging was against the law of the land, plain and simple," Teresa answered soberly. "We didn't need that huge, fine house in town. We were as happy as could be out on the ranch. Ice skating on the Little Goose Creek in the wintertime and running through the hills in the summer. It was striving after riches that took my father down that path and then led to J.B.'s death. Now J.B. is all alone, buried in the Twin Falls Cemetery. Come to think of it, he does have a marble angel sitting on his headstone, which is comforting."

Christine remembered her mom's faraway look by the fire that time. No picture or story from her brothers could have given Christine that memory of her mother. She knew Teresa resented her father's sin, but she also knew that her mother felt like she had inherited her father's mischievous streak. Why did Teresa resent leaving the ranch for more money, but then essentially do the same thing with her own family when Patrick came along?

They all loved life on Deep Creek in the summers and then their sweet little house in Delta City during the school year. Why did they eventually leave the house and go live in an old hotel in Cedarville for the winters? Why did she want to give up their summers in the woods? Maybe Teresa got scared by the mountain lion near camp, or by Samuel falling from the tree. She was certain he had busted his appendix—like J.B.

There was also the time Christine almost fell over a cliff when she leaned against the flimsy wall of the boys' fort—built across the creek and next to the ledge. Teresa would always tease that Francis was her favorite son since he had caught Christine in time. Even so, maybe Teresa was frightened enough to make a significant life change.

Or maybe there was a limit to her strength and vitality? Teresa had come down with Hepatitis and was ordered to drink high-protein drinks and have complete rest. "I just thought I had a nice golden tan and had finally lost those stubborn five pounds." Teresa had laughed. Maybe it was a combination of all those events that pushed Teresa into Patrick's arms and a life of prestige. Teresa had resented that weakness in her father, but then had caved in the same way.

Christine thought again about the sins of the fathers and mothers being passed down, and she felt dread in her stomach. She prayed again and tried to focus on that sweet smell of the water. She closed her eyes, and she could remember skinny dipping with her family in Deep Creek. Of course, her mother made the boys turn away while the girls got in the water. There was so much laughter, splashing, and merriment.

"God, please take me back to that joy and peace," Christine prayed aloud. "We felt it then. It was all so simple. But then life got in the way. I know that the only lasting joy and peace can be found with you, though. I don't want to continue the generational sins of my family. I want to live for you. Please help me."

Christine had an impulse to get in the water then, like the old days. They were always skinny-dipping while she was growing up. That may be strange for some, but not for their family. Christine looked around to double-check, but, as usual, no one was there, and the foliage around the creek was very thick.

It wasn't just a dip that Christine wanted, though. She wanted to be cleansed of generational sin, the world's dirtiness, and the sordid paths of her ancestors. Christine longed for purity.

"I know I can't baptize myself, and I have already been baptized," Christine thought to herself as she quickly undressed. "But I have heard of other churches doing baptisms in the creek or the river, and it sounds so cleansing and powerful."

She stepped into the creek and caught her breath with the chill. "It's freezing!" Christine said out loud. "This reminds me of the old days. Cold water never stopped us." She quickly submerged herself and gave a little shout, like her mother always did, except this time she shouted, "In the name of the Father!" Then she submerged herself twice more for the Son, and then for the Holy Spirit. Then she kept talking out loud, as if in prayer. "God, this is so refreshing and freeing. Nothing smells better than this water, and I feel like you gave me a gift with that sweet scent just now. God, I know I shouldn't call this a baptism, but it feels like one to me. I want to remember this day and this place forever. And I want to ask you to save me from the generational sin of my family. The bootlegging, sneaking, lying, and my dad's alcoholism. Please help me with whatever is happening back home, with Patrick, and with my mom. I know another divorce is not ideal, but I can't help but want Patrick out of the picture. He isn't nice to me, Samuel, or my mother either. Please take us back to the old days, God. If that is even possible."

The mist had finally burned off, and the sun was shining brightly through the trees. The sun's rays felt so warm as Christine climbed out and quickly rubbed herself down with her clothes. As she was dressing, she began singing a song her grammar school teacher used to sing with them. The light made her think of it. "The darkness soon shall flee valleys in shadow, sunlight I can foresee…"

Her teacher, Mrs. Monroe, got the grammar school classes together for a Christmas performance each year right before school let out for the holidays. The story of Saint Lucia was her favorite, and Christine began to recall the year Mrs. Monroe chose her to play Saint Lucia herself. This was such an honor, and her mother had been thrilled. Of course, she had cut Christine's bangs short again right before the performance, and Christine was mortified. Thankfully, the crown with the candles covered them up, and Christine was at peace again.

You had to be at peace to play the part of Saint Lucia. She was light and peace herself because God had given her His light and peace. Christine could barely sleep the night before the performance. Teresa had taken it upon herself to bake three batches of her seven-layer cookies and to wrap dozens of small presents. Saint Lucia always handed out treats and presents. Christine was beginning to worry about that because it would take forever to hand out everything her mother was preparing. "It will be ok, it will be ok," Christine kept repeating to herself.

It was especially exciting that year because her little brother, Patrick Jr., was old enough to dress up as a gingerbread child. Christine had been a gingerbread child in the past years. She remembered the years when her older brothers got to wear the pointed hats with golden stars for the performance. Of course, her stepfather would finally come to the performance since one of his own children would be in it. Rather than let Christine and Patrick, Jr. wear the worn-out costumes from past years, Teresa had insisted on making new ones. Christine's pristine, white robe gleamed. The red sash she would wear across the front was wide and very expensive. The best part was that Christine would wear the honored crown with seven new candles burning. And, again, her horrid haircut would be covered.

"God is wherever you let God in," Christine repeated again the night before as she finally began to drift off to sleep. "Saint Lucia, please pray for me. I don't want to embarrass you tomorrow."

Christine thought back to the pageant and willed herself to focus on the good moments as she sang, "Though long may be the night, hope, she is bringing, hear now, the maid in white, silently winging, hushed wonder in the air, lights glowing in her hair, Santa Lucia! Santa Lucia!"

What could ever paint a more lovely picture than the thought of the pure maiden, Lucia, who would rather help fellow believers living in the catacombs than marry? Saint Lucia's hands had to be free to help, so she lit her way with candles placed on her head.

That night at the pageant, Christine tried to block everything from her mind except her task at hand. It could have been embarrassing to have a seemingly endless supply of treats and gifts to hand out, but Christine didn't let that bother her. She ignored her mother's words to her before the pageant, "All the other mothers are going to envy you in this beautiful costume, Chrissy!" Christine also put away the thought of Patrick being there, gloating over only his own flesh and blood, without a thought of her.

Of course, Christine couldn't have been more pleased to have Patrick Jr. there as the cutest gingerbread boy that ever walked the earth. He was simply a cherub, and she loved her little brother dearly. But that night, her thoughts were wholly immersed in her role as Saint Lucia, as if the lives of all believers depended on her light and provision.

"The darkness soon shall flee valleys in shadow, sunlight I can foresee, over, over the meadows, the sun will come again! Rise in the sky to reign! Santa Lucia! Santa Lucia!"

There at Dochero, with her senses clear after her dip in the cold water, Christine repeated those words again out loud— "The darkness soon shall flee valleys in shadow, sunlight I can foresee, over, over the meadows, the sun will come again!"

Chapter 21

"Anne!" Matthew reprimanded his wife on the narrow bridge overlooking the creek that morning. "This is not appropriate!"

"Oh, come on, Matthew, haven't you ever heard of skinny dipping?" Anne couldn't help but giggle then as she looked at her husband before continuing. "It's as old as the sun. Of course, not everyone was openly skinny-dipping in the '60s, but it caught on again soon after. But what struck me that morning was that it seemed to be a spiritual experience for Christine—as I mentioned, like a baptism of sorts."

Edward's mind had wandered, and he was far from shocked. The Murphy family had talked openly of skinny dipping. Edward remembered how Teresa had teased him in front of her family at one of their dinners.

"You have never heard of skinny dipping, have you, Father Edward?" she had asked him with that now familiar twinkle in her eyes.

Edward had nearly choked as he looked around the table at Murph, Francis, Joseph, and little Anthony with his big, cherubic eyes. "You are right, I have never heard of it. In Ohio, even the men put on about three layers of swimming clothes before getting into the water. It was actually rare to swim, in fact. One of my aunts was a very strict nun, and she always insisted that the boys and girls never swim at the same time."

The whole table erupted in laughter then. Francis spoke up, "We all skinny dip often in the summers up north, even Mom and Dad. We practically live in the woods when we are up there. I can't wait to go back. This will be the first summer that Anthony is old enough to enjoy it. You are excited, aren't you, Anthony?"

It looked like Anthony could barely contain his excitement.

Edward remembered a feeling of heaviness then. The real truth was that he had never learned to swim, let alone skinny dip. After George's death, Edward's parents didn't want Edward anywhere near the water. A feeling of loneliness and alienation swept over him—he knew it would be lonely when the Murphys left for the summer. He had become so accustomed to feeling like one of them.

"You should drive up and serve Mass in the mountains and see us!" Teresa suggested. "Murph would come and pick you up, but he isn't allowed to leave the area. A fight might erupt over water rights, and in the past, those fights have sometimes turned into killings. The water there is like liquid gold. That's another reason we like skinny-dipping. I will be so big and pregnant by the time summer is over, I will surely need help climbing in and out of the water."

Everyone laughed at the thought, and Edward just shook his head, as if to dislodge his thoughts.

When Edward said goodnight that evening, he expressed gratitude for being invited to serve Mass up there, but it wasn't his decision where he went for Mass. It was up to the bishop.

"We will all miss you, won't we, boys?" Teresa had said as they walked out onto the front porch. Murph had fallen asleep on the couch. "Do take care of yourself, Father Edward. I imagine you will be very lonely without us. Hopefully, we will all be ok up there in the wilds. Murph is drinking so much these days that we can't really rely on him. A lot of the ranchers check in on us, though, don't they, Francis?"

Edward looked over to see Francis watching his mother with a suspicious look.

"Wow, Mom, you really went big with the Estée Lauder tonight."

Teresa laughed, "I do like to leave what they call a 'lasting impression.'"

Edward's feelings were all over the place that night. First, he felt concern for the little family up in 'the wilds' as Teresa had called it. Then he felt jealous upon hearing that all the ranchers were checking in. Was Teresa doing that on purpose? He was definitely slow where women were concerned, but nothing about Teresa was slow.

"Will you worry, Father? Will you miss us?" Teresa grabbed his hand and looked up at him. Edward found himself staring at her mouth. It wasn't like the tense, thin-lipped mouths of the women he was accustomed to meeting.

"Well, uh, of course I will miss your whole family. I will be praying for you. Especially since you will be so close to your delivery time." Edward withdrew his hand from hers. "Good night, may God bless you all."

"Father Edward? Father Edward? May we go down to the creek now?"

It was Margaret's voice that brought Edward back to the present.

"Yes, of course. I am not sure where my mind went."

"We know where it went," Matthew spoke up. "How could it not go there with Anne talking the way she was?"

"I don't think the Father heard what I said," Anne changed the conversation again. "I had said that Christine was singing some sort of song while she was down in the water. It was something like, 'light over the meadows and the sunshine coming again.' Even through the trees, I could see that Christine was almost glowing. You all probably won't believe me, but maybe there is something special about this place. I guess we will find out. I hope it is special for Andrew, like it was for her."

Edward spoke up, "It sounds like she was singing about Saint Lucia. The feast of Saint Lucia is a cherished feast. Remind me to tell you about it someday."

"It is special, isn't it, Father Edward?" Margaret interrupted. "This place? I have seen the way you pray down here, in our Dochero."

"Don't use that word," Matthew snapped as he made his way down the little trail. "It gives me the creeps."

Everyone grew silent as they made their way down to the creek, and Edward began to pray to himself. "God, please help us. Please, that little Andrew would be healed and would be able to shine your light to the world. Saint Lucia, you did not hide your light under a bushel, but let it shine for the whole world, for all the centuries to see. We may not suffer torture in our lives the way you did, but we are still called to let the light

190

of our Christianity illuminate our daily lives. Please pray for us to have the courage to bring our Christianity into every corner of our day—our work, our recreation, our relationships, our conversation. And please pray for the healing of little Andrew—just as your eyes were miraculously restored. Amen."

Edward looked up to see the family staring at him expectantly.

"So what is your big plan?" Matthew asked.

Anne reprimanded him. "Please, Matthew. Don't say it like that. We agreed to bring Andrew here in the hope that this special place might have the healing powers of God. Please pray in your heart to God for that and pray for Father Edward."

"Yes, please pray for me." Edward echoed. "Well, let's see, Andrew expressed wanting to be baptized, and I would like to hear his reasons."

Everyone turned to Andrew. Matthew had leaned Andrew, in his brace, up against a rock at the water's edge.

Andrew hesitated a moment, but then spoke up loud and clear. "Well, you all worry about me all of the time, and I don't want you to be sad. It worries me to see you all so stressed. But I wanted you to know that I am not sad about myself. This is me, and this is all I have ever known. I'm not unhappy. It is all of you who are unhappy. When I am stuck in a brace all of the time, and can't go out and do all of the things that other kids are doing, it makes me know that the peace and joy I feel must come from God. It isn't like I am feeling joy from going outside, running around, and laughing with others. There is no mistake that it is from God. God talks to me sometimes, in the silence, or it is more like He whispers to me. Things like, 'It is alright, Andrew. You are my precious lamb. I want you to tell others about me.' Things like that. I want to be baptized as a way to say thank you to God. I want you all to really understand that I am ok. God has me. It is you that I am worried about. My biggest prayers are always for you."

Edward noticed that Anne, Margaret, and Matthew seemed to be at a loss for words as they listened to Andrew.

Matthew finally spoke up, "I have never heard you speak that many words in your whole life."

"He talks that way to me all of the time," Margaret said.

Anne added, "I am sorry we have worried you, Andrew. We just want the best for you."

"And that is what we are going to pray for today, in these baptismal waters," Edward said as he sat down to remove his shoes and socks. "We are going to pray for whatever is God's best for Andrew."

"This is all a bunch of hogwash," Matthew was acting uneasy again.

Anne put her hand on his arm, "Please, Matthew. We made it this far."

Edward stood and spoke up, "First, I would like to bless the waters."

Edward reached into his pocket and pulled out a vial of oil. Edward crossed himself and said, "In the name of the Father, and of the Son, and of the Holy Spirit." Removing the cap, he sprinkled the oil over the creek and continued, "That through his Son the power of the Holy Spirit may be sent upon the water, so that he who is baptized may be 'born of water and the Spirit.'"

Then Edward turned to Andrew. "Are you ready, little chap?" he asked.

Andrew nodded, and Edward went over, knelt down, and removed his shoes and socks, too. "Let's pray that we don't catch our death with the cold. And can I tell you a secret?" Andrew nodded again before Edward continued in a whisper, "I don't know how to swim."

Andrew laughed loudly, "That's ok, the water is shallow and I'll protect you. It will be fun. I am usually not allowed to be this adventurous."

"Ok, if you say so. Here we go," Edward said, lifting Andrew and carrying him into the water. "First, I am going to pray to cast the devil clean out of your life. In the name of the Father, and of the Son, and of the Holy Spirit." Edward made the cross over Andrew before continuing. "Almighty and ever living God, you sent your only Son into the world to cast out the power of Satan, spirit of evil, to rescue man from the kingdom of darkness, and bring him into the splendor of your kingdom of light. We pray for Andrew. Set him free from original sin, make him a temple of your glory, and send your Holy Spirit to dwell within him. We ask this through Christ our Lord."

Edward turned toward Matthew, Anne, and Margaret and held his hand up over them. "You have come here to present Andrew for baptism. By water and the Holy Spirit, he is to receive the gift of new life from God, who is Love. On your part, you must make it your constant care to bring Andrew up in the practice of the faith. See that the divine life which God gives him is kept safe from the poison of sin, to grow always stronger in his heart. If your faith makes you ready to accept this responsibility, renew now your vows of your own baptism. Reject sin; profess your faith in Christ Jesus. This is the faith of the church. This is the faith in which Andrew is about to be baptized."

"Do you commit to this?" Edward asked them.

"We do," Anne answered before nudging Matthew and Margaret. "We do," They said.

Edward led them all in the Confession of Faith.

"Ok, here we go, Andrew. Hold your breath." Edward dunked him under one time, "In the name of the Father…"

Andrew sputtered but then immediately regained his smile.

"In the name of the Son." Edward put him under again.

"In the name of the Holy Spirit." Edward dunked Andrew one last time before saying, "Amen."

Andrew was thoroughly wet and cold, but his smile lit up his whole face. Anne was wiping tears from her eyes. She held open a towel, and Edward handed Andrew into her embrace.

Edward reached out and touched Andrew's ears and then his mouth as he prayed, "The Lord Jesus made the deaf hear and the dumb speak. May He soon touch your ears to receive His word and your mouth to proclaim His faith to the praise and glory of God the Father."

Moving his hand to Andrew's back, Edward added his own prayer, "God of mercy, if you would see fit to bring healing also to Andrew's back that he may use a strong and straight body to serve you in this life. Amen."

He stepped back and motioned to all, "Let us recite the Lord's prayer together."

This brought tears to Edward's eyes—the communal prayer to God, recited for thousands of years. "Please, God," Edward prayed quietly. "Please, that this family would commit their lives fully to you."

Edward turned to Matthew and said, "I would like to say one more prayer, please." Edward put his hand on Matthew's arm, and he could feel Matthew shift in annoyance. Edward wiped his own eyes and pushed his glasses up his nose before looking into Matthew's eyes. Edward closed his eyes and said, "God is the giver of all life, human and divine. May

He bless you as Andrew's father. With Anne, you will be the first teachers of Andrew and Margaret in the ways of faith. May you also be the best teachers, bearing witness to the faith by what you say and do, in Christ Jesus our Lord."

Edward looked up into Matthew's eyes, and it felt like they were boring into his own soul. "Forgive me, God," Edward whispered.

"What did you just say?" Matthew asked in anger.

Edward ignored him, turning to Anne and Andrew then. "Are you going to be warm enough, Andrew?"

Andrew nodded and continued to smile. "I feel great!"

"Do you?" Matthew demanded. "This was all just a bunch of fiddle faddle. Let me look at you, Andrew."

Matthew grabbed Andrew from Anne. "Let's see if you can stand after being in those blessed waters."

Anne cried out, "Matthew, don't!"

Matthew threw the towel down, and, with his clinging, wet clothing, Edward could see just how frail and small Andrew was. Andrew's countenance was serene, despite the contention.

"Show us, Andrew. Show us how strong you are." Matthew continued while Anne openly sobbed.

Matthew set Andrew on his feet and then let go. Andrew wobbled momentarily before falling forward. Margaret jumped in and grabbed him.

"It's ok, Andrew. You will get stronger, just trust God."

"I do trust Him," Andrew replied, leaning his head against Margaret's shoulder.

"We are done here," Matthew said. He scooped up Andrew with one arm and then grabbed the brace with his other hand. "We are leaving. Thanks for nothing, Father Edward."

"I'm sorry, Father. Thank you," Anne said, looking back as she grabbed Andrew's socks and shoes and then followed her husband up the hill.

Margaret put her hand on Edward's arm and looked up at him. "I'm sorry, too, Father Edward. I know you tried your best. I hope we didn't ruin Dochero for you."

"Of course, you didn't. You'd better go now," he said to her.

Margaret took off at a run and then stopped on the bridge to look down at him. She gave a little wave.

Edward lifted his hand and then let it drop to his side.

"This disaster is my fault alone," he thought to himself. "I am a total hypocrite before God and before that family, and they know it."

Edward sat down and put his socks and shoes back on. His vestments and pant legs were wet and had accumulated some dirt on their hems. He removed his glasses and wiped his eyes and nose with his arm. He felt so low. He wanted to crush his glasses and throw them in the creek. He wanted to throw himself in the creek and get washed away with it, forever.

He put his head in his hands and let the grief overcome him. He quoted Elijah from the time he sat against a broom bush, "'I have had enough, Lord,' he said. 'Take my life; I am no better than my ancestors.'"

Edward shivered, and his teeth began to chatter. The whole scenario made him feel like a child again. Some of Andrew's words came back to him then, "God has His best for me. I know that. Even if he doesn't heal me, it's my father that I am worried about."

"This is my fault, God," Edward said out loud. "It would have been nice if you had healed Andrew for his dad's sake, but you are probably trying to teach me a lesson, too. I get it. I think I know what I need to do."

Edward stood up and brushed himself off. He was glad it was Saturday and that Alice had the whole day off with her mother in Nevada City. The thought of going back and having a cigarette only lasted a moment. Edward had learned that prostrations or a brisk walk would help to drive that temptation away. "Thank you, God, for helping me with the urge for a cigarette or to go buy a bottle of wine. Not to mention drinking the communion wine. I am so ashamed of those days, God. Please have mercy on me."

Edward picked up the pace and set his face like flint. He knew exactly what he needed to do. When he got back to the rectory, he thanked God again for Alice's absence. He just needed time alone to focus.

After removing his vestments and changing pants, Edward yanked open his nightstand drawer. The sound of the contents shifting noisily was somehow satisfying. "If my life were represented by material things, this is it." Edward thought.

Edward, for a moment, bypassed his original intent and grabbed the stack of photographs. He quickly shuffled past the ones of his family and his time in seminary. He paused momentarily at one of the pictures of himself and Billy Sunday. It gave him strength and inspiration to see it. He hoped that Billy would approve of his plan. Sometimes you have to stop worrying about what people will think. You just have to do what the Lord would ask of you.

Edward found the picture he was looking for. It was the only one of Christine that he had kept in this pile. It was the picture of Christine when she had played the part of Saint Lucia. She looked like an absolute angel, with a crown of candles on her head and a robe so shiny and white that it glowed. She wasn't smiling really. The look on her face was one of resolve, as if she had set her face like flint to fulfill her purpose. The words of the song came to Edward then,

"The darkness soon shall flee valleys in shadow, sunlight I can foresee, over, over the meadows, the sun will come again."

"Yes, it is sunlight that I can foresee," Edward said quietly. "Thank you, God, for bringing me out of my despair so quickly and for giving me a purpose."

Edward grabbed his wallet, car keys, and the lone key before shutting the drawer.

Chapter 22

The money owed to Mt. St. Paul's was apparently paid, and Teresa came to collect Christine early on a Friday morning. When her mother came bursting through the doors, like a warm spring breeze, Christine felt a rush of love toward her—like she had been homesick but hadn't realized it. Teresa caught Christine in a tight embrace and said, "Let's get you out of here."

Christine glanced over to see Sister Mary Rita eyeing them suspiciously. Then she spoke up, "May I speak with you for a moment, Mrs. Harrison?"

Teresa acted like she didn't hear her. She pulled out of the embrace to look at Christine and exclaim, "Guess what? The Beatles are coming to the Cow Palace for their very first United States tour—and I got tickets! Aunt Virginia is friends with the mayor, you know, so she was able to help get them! We are going to have to practically turn around and come right back down here, but you know I don't mind the drive! Won't it be fun?"

Christine was dumbfounded. "My mom is superwoman," she thought.

They heard Sister Mary Rita clear her throat.

Teresa looked at Christine and said, "Would you take some of this out to the car while I speak with Sister Mary Rita?"

Christine hesitated a moment and then said, "Alright." She wondered what needed to be said between them. Maybe Sister Mary Rita wanted to tell her mother about the underwear incident during the school's centennial celebration or the time Christine had socked Sandra and given her a bloody nose after Sandra had teased her one too many times. Sandra used to go on about how the other girls received more letters and phone calls from home, and that Christine's family must not care about her. Christine's brothers were always punching each other, but Christine didn't know she had it in her. Sister Mary Rita had only given her a long sideways glance but had said nothing else. Christine thought that the school staff was secretly pleased and that Sandra had it coming. Well, maybe Sister Mary Rita had decided to tell her mother all, and Christine figured she deserved it.

As Christine put her things in their car, she glanced over at St. Clement's across the street. Since they had their own chapel at the school, the boarders didn't have much to do with St. Clement's, beyond Sunday Mass. But it was all a familiar and beautiful sight—the steepled church at the end of the narrow street with its cemetery nestled amongst the pines and gentle, rolling hills.

Christine saw movement as she surveyed the church grounds. A young woman was watching her, and she recalled other times she had seen the same woman watching her. Christine decided to try to talk to her.

"Hello?" She called out as she crossed the narrow street. "What is your name?"

The woman disappeared behind the church, and Christine tried to follow her. Passing several statues, Christine walked between the rectory and the parish hall. She saw the woman enter one of the small houses behind the rectory.

"Oh well," Christine sighed to herself.

As Christine turned to leave, the strong scent of lilac overtook her, and she glanced around, looking for the source. She spotted the lilac near the rectory's back door and went to it. She wasn't sure what possessed her, but she sat down next to it on the back step.

"I don't think anything could smell more heavenly than this," Christine said out loud. She pulled a branch close to her, heavy with blossom, and sank her face into it. It was still wet with morning dew, and Christine savored the coolness against her face. She looked up and saw the woman watching her through her window. Christine gave her a wave and a smile before she jumped up. The woman returned the wave but didn't smile.

"Well, that was a sweet parting gift," Christine thought to herself. "Another corner of the world that I will savor in my memory—the back porch step, a fragrant lilac bush, and a wave from a neighbor. She seems unhappy, so I think I will remember her in my prayers."

"Chrissy? Chrissy?" Christine could hear Teresa calling to her from across the street. Impulsively, Christine turned back and twisted a branch off the lilac bush to take with her. "A memento," she thought. "That way I will remember to pray for that woman."

"Here I come, Mom!" Christine ran across the street. She settled herself, breathlessly, in the front passenger seat.

Teresa turned to her and said, "Could you please dispose of that? The scent of it may overtake me."

"How about I put it in the trunk. I want to keep it as a memento." Christine jumped out and opened the trunk, laying the flower on one of her suitcases.

"We do have lilacs in Alturas, you know!" Teresa yelled.

"I know!" Christine yelled back. "But this one is special," she whispered to herself.

As she climbed back into the car, she asked, "What was all of that about with Sister Mary Rita?"

"Oh, it was nothing. We were just making sure the accounts were all settled. Why, is there something you are hiding from me?" Teresa looked over and winked.

Christine could tell that she was changing the subject, but, in an unusual wave of talkativeness, she told her mom all her wild tales.

"I am certainly proud of you, Chrissy. I knew that you didn't fall far from this old tree." Teresa laughed. "You had mentioned punching that girl and breaking her shampoo bottle in one of your letters home. It sounds like you saved everyone from further grief from her. Now, the underwear incident. Wow! Your brothers are going to love that story."

Immediately, Christine felt ashamed. She wasn't really proud of her escapades. Maybe she had wanted her mother's approval, but now she regretted it.

"Can we keep that to ourselves, please, Mom? I am not really proud of that. As much as the school had its faults, it had a lot to offer as well."

"Oh, that's right, you did mention that they rarely turned the heat on and that the food was horrid." Teresa smiled over at her again, "And you said that all the boarders were crummy, wayward people…"

"That's enough, please. I must have been in a mood when I wrote that." Christine slouched down even further in her seat. She didn't like to think of herself as a complainer, and her mom seemed to relish remembering everything she had said and done. Christine felt bad that she had said such things about Julie, who had later died. "There was so much to be thankful for, and I must have been trying to sound dramatic. Can I have those letters back when I get home? I think I'd like to burn them."

"Don't worry, I already did. They are long gone." Teresa glanced over at Christine. "Why that look? You know how I don't like to hang on to stuff. Believe me, I memorized every word and read them out loud to the family before I got rid of them."

"Great!" Christine exclaimed. Her talkative spell was long over, and now she felt depressed.

Teresa picked up the conversation, "Well, I am sorry to bring up unpleasant stuff so soon, but I wanted to let you know that I have filed for divorce from Patrick." Teresa looked over as if to assess Christine's reaction.

Christine just stared straight ahead at the road.

"Why the silence? You never liked him, and I'm sorry to say, he never liked you. That's no secret. I'm not sure why, really. Maybe because I spoiled you so much—you were my first girl, after all. What did he expect? I really can't pinpoint it. Sometimes I think it's just because you are special. Remember how I mentioned your French ancestors and clairvoyance? It's almost like God made you special like them. Something about you just really got under Patrick's fingernails. Maybe it was nothing more than you not being his own flesh and blood."

"Great." Christine thought to herself. "It's true that Patrick never liked me, but it doesn't feel good to hear it again. And I don't even want to think about that clairvoyance stuff—it sounds creepy."

"We were waiting until you got home for the divorce proceedings. I need you to testify about how he treated you and the times you and I drove around looking for signs of his running around.

Christine wanted to die. What a way to end her year at Mt. St. Paul's.

"Can you please just take me back?" Teresa gave a start at Christine's sudden exuberance. "Can you please just beg Sister Mary Rita to let me live there for the summer? I'll be a nun or whatever she wants me to be. A life of religious service would be much better than dealing with all of this garbage."

Teresa stared at Christine like she was from another planet and then said, "You have circles under your eyes. What has gotten into you? This isn't like you, but I guess I shouldn't be surprised."

"What do you mean, you shouldn't be surprised? Please don't bring up the French ancestors again."

Teresa seemed at a loss for words, but then she said, "I just mean that I shouldn't be surprised that the nuns had an influence on you this past year. Sister Mary Rita did say that you were definitely set apart from the rest—the way you went to chapel every morning and seemed to take a lot of time to be contemplative. They said that being contemplative is a sign of spiritual maturity. That is why they didn't put much weight into your minor infractions."

"I don't think dishonoring the school on their biggest celebration was a minor infraction. I deserved punishment. I am really tired of all this special treatment. During my so-called contemplations, I realized just how spoiled I have been my whole life, and I really want to know why." Christine was surprised by her own outburst, since she had recently realized how much she admired and loved her mother. The talk of another divorce and chaos must have been a breaking point.

Teresa looked flustered, which was unusual for her. She was usually in command of every situation. She looked at Christine again before continuing. "Well, if you must know. You were a miracle child. There is no other explanation for it. I don't like to talk badly about your father, Murph, but he really had slipped quite low into his alcoholism. The boys were finding him passed out on the floor, and he was absent when I needed him most. You know I almost died with Samuel's birth, and he almost died, too. I couldn't believe how much blood I lost." Teresa shuddered before continuing. "It made me very low for a long time, and I had trouble recovering. If I asked Murph to help, he would stomp around and grumble, and I fell into a deep depression." Teresa searched Christine's face, almost like she needed her approval.

"I eventually had to ask Murph to move out. If it wasn't for the church being nearly next door, I don't know if I would have made it. The church ladies were always helping, and one of the assistant pastors was very attentive. He was friends with Murph, so he felt obligated to look after us. The one thing I could still manage was to bake cookies for the various church groups. You know how much I liked making those seven-layer cookies! Father Ed, I mean, the assistant pastor liked them, too."

"Oh, were you going to say Father Edward? I remember him from the time you took me to see him after Georgia died. On my first night at Mt. St. Paul's, I wondered if anyone had ever prayed for me, and later I remembered that Father Edward said he would always pray for me. It is so nice to know I have someone praying for me."

Teresa looked flustered and said, "What a silly thought. You don't think I pray for you? I always say my prayers."

Christine thought her mother was acting very strange as she went back to telling her story.

"Well, anyway, I just had a major hormonal imbalance, and I knew if I had any more children, I probably wouldn't make it. Murph insisted I go see a psychiatrist, which I did. The psychiatrist said that my life was really off-balance. Everyone is supposed to have an equal measure of work, faith, play, and love. He said I was really low on play. I tried to look for ways to have fun. I took what he said very seriously. I even thought the answer might be to let Murph move back in—so I did— before he had to go back up to the mountains for his water job. I figured it would give us a short trial to see if he had improved. So that's when I got pregnant with you, a true miracle."

Christine felt sick even to imagine that. "Ok, that's enough, Mom."

"No, I'm sorry, but you have to let me finish. I have never told anyone this. I actually thought of aborting you." She looked over at Christine then.

Christine didn't know what to say.

"Isn't that awful? Please forgive me. It just shows what a mess I was—in my mind, my body, and my marriage, because it turns out that you were an absolute angel in my life. A true miracle. I finally got my girl. Murph called you his Irish lass and proudly told all of his priest friends that you were 99% Irish. Don't you see what a miracle it was for you to be born? If I hadn't let Murph come home for that little bit…"

"It's ok, Mom. No need to get yourself worked up. I understand now. That gives me a lot to think about. Thank you."

"I know I don't tell you often how much I love you, but I do love you with all of my heart, and I will be so glad to have you home." Teresa reached over and squeezed Christine's hand. "And don't worry, we get to go to the Beatles concert before the court date."

After that, much of the trip was in silence, and they decided to make the whole trip in one day. There wasn't a celebratory feeling, like usual. A somber task lay ahead of them all.

When they reached home late that night, Christine told her mother she wanted to go straight to bed and sleep until late the next morning.

Teresa replied, "I will try to hold the little ones back, but they will sure be anxious to see you." She followed Christine to her bedroom.

When Christine opened her door and turned on the light, she was greeted by a stunning sight. Her whole room had been completely redecorated and updated. Canopies had been attached to the twin beds. The golden wallpaper was replaced with a pale yellow pattern, and new, white chenille coverlets and cushions adorned the beds.

Her mom stepped next to her in the doorframe.

"What do you think? I wanted it to be ready so that you can start having sleepovers."

"Oh, Mom! I don't know what to say. I am so sorry for how crabby I have been toward you today." Christine pulled Teresa close. "And I love you, too. I didn't say it earlier, but during some of my time at school, I realized how much I love and admire you. I am sorry for not saying it more." Christine surveyed the room again and said, "This is just so beautiful— I can't believe my eyes. Can we please wake the girls now and let them be my first sleepover in my new room?"

"They have been sleeping with me since Patrick has been gone, but I can go wake them." Teresa looked a little forlorn.

"No, it's ok. How about we both just go crawl in with them? We wouldn't want to mess up more beds!"

"I don't know what to say," Teresa answered. "You are just my miracle, that's all. And now I will have all of my girls in one place."

Christine got ready in a flash and crawled in next to Abigail, nudging her slightly toward Maggie in the middle. She loved her little sisters so much. Christine snuggled in next to them and then heard a small voice in the doorway. It was Patrick Jr., "I want to sleep with Chrissy, too." Christine waved him over and tucked him in next to her side—relishing in the feeling of togetherness.

Just as Christine's eyes were growing heavy with sleep, she looked over and saw Teresa kneeling in prayer at the edge of the bed, surrounded by the glow of a lamp, and heard soft murmurings as she prayed through her list.

Chapter 23

Feeling thankful to be free of obligations for a few hours, Edward left the house and fired up his old Pontiac. It had been a gift from his grandfather before he died, and while Edward was still in seminary. Lately, he had forgotten just how much he enjoyed taking it for a drive. He had driven it cross-country on several occasions, and those trips were highlights for him. Years ago, when he heard that Meadowbrook was seeking a resident pastor to build its new church, Edward put his name forward as a candidate. One of his motives was to have the chance to drive his car more often in a rural setting. He had rarely been able to take it out while living in Delta City. Starting a church in Meadowbrook would fulfill his dream of becoming a missionary priest in the West, and he would have rural parishioners to visit with his car.

That is also one of the reasons he had come to love Pine Valley and, Lord willing, he planned to finish out his ministry here. Now that the Lord had freed him from the rut that he was in with all the drinking, smoking, and hiding, Edward wanted to start fresh—visiting people in the outlying areas would help, even if he had to pay for gas out of his own pocket. He was even considering starting up a radio program, as he had done in Meadowbrook, to reach people for Christ. The station could play episodes of "Unshackled," from Pacific Garden Mission.

On that day, firing up the old Pontiac, Edward felt the enthusiasm that he hadn't felt since just after seminary. First things first, though—Edward was on a mission to go to the bank and open up his safety deposit box. He could have walked, but the car had been sitting for far too long.

Edward felt a little sheepish for having to keep a safety deposit box, but, before the Bishop, and most importantly, before God, his reasons were pure. He didn't want to fuel the gossip mill by keeping it all at the house, with the chance that the housekeeper might stumble upon it. He just wanted to protect the innocent and not cause anyone to stumble.

Once he retrieved the wooden box of contents from the safety deposit box, Edward went out to his car and decided to take a little drive. He followed Highway 20 to a dirt road that led to a mountain stream surrounded by quaking aspens. This was his favorite spot to take a drive. It reminded him of the time that he drove north to see the Murphy family, as Teresa had suggested. Those were still good times, before things took a turn. Bishop Brown needed to check on the priest in Alturas, and he suggested that Edward go along. Edward was thrilled to offer to drive the bishop in his car. The high desert region was a new experience for Edward at the time. He wasn't sure how he felt about the sagebrush flats, but he was instantly enamored with the quaking aspen as they headed over Cedar Pass.

"Yes, this area is a lot like Cedar Pass. It refreshes my soul," Edward thought while he sat in his car. He rolled down the window so he could hear the stream and the quaking leaves. Only then did he open the wooden box and begin looking through the contents. He pulled out a stack of pictures. Edward had told Teresa to stop sending them, but she had persisted. He had to keep a post office box just for that reason. She would stop at nothing to track him down, so it was just easier to give her each new address.

Always one to keep things in order, Edward first looked at the pictures of when he had met the Murphy family. There was a photo of himself with Francis and Joseph when they first wore their altar server cassocks. "They were such fine boys, full of life," Edward thought. "Always joking around and so bright. They could really fight, too. Teresa had written once that Joseph had taken a knife and stabbed Francis in the rear." Edward laughed to himself. Then there was a picture of Anthony, like a little cherub in his cassock. Edward had really bonded with Anthony since he was born soon after he first met the Murphys. He really liked to cuddle up to Edward those days and talk about God. Edward had a feeling that Anthony might want to be a priest one day, but in her letters, Teresa had proudly told him that Anthony had become a doctor.

There were several pictures of Edward and Murph together. "God bless him," Edward said. He had many letters from Murph in the box as well. They had stayed in touch. "It is really too bad how everything went downhill there for a while," Edward reminisced. "I think he and Teresa could have made it with more time. Teresa insisted that she had married for life, just like her parents had. The birth of Samuel just put her out of her mind for a while. It was the only time in her whole life that she had lost command of the situation."

Edward reached the picture of when he and the bishop had driven to see the Murphys. Each summer, the Murphys had rented a charming house on the edge of town, and there was a picture of all of them in front of it. Teresa was very advanced in her pregnancy. She had been told that she was carrying Samuel "frank breech," a difficult position, and there was underlying stress. Her eyes did look weary, and her smile wasn't quite as vibrant. Little Anthony clung to Edward's leg in the picture, and that sight is what first brought the tears to Edward's eyes. Anthony was such a little angel, he remembered again. There was so much love between Teresa and her sons. That summer was hard on Teresa. Murph had gotten in trouble with his boss for taking off with the resident priest to go drinking down in Chico. This is why Bishop Brown was making frequent visits to the area. It was easy to see that a small fissure had begun in their marriage, and, in hindsight, there was going to be no stopping the break.

This made Edward so sad. After their divorce, it didn't take long for Murph to give up drinking entirely and dedicate his life to God. He had become a successful toy inventor and lived in Anaheim. If they could have just waited it out, he could have been a father to those boys and even to Christine, whom Murph adored. They could have waited out the crisis and forgiven each other. Edward blew his nose. Edward believed in marriage. Just like in the priesthood, or with any calling in life, one must endure the dark night of the soul and push on. Every day is a chance to battle the flesh and be victorious with the help of Christ.

But how could he blame Murph and Teresa? Edward had been young and foolish right along with them. And surely his own sin had not helped the situation. "God forgive me," Edward said out loud.

There was a picture then of Teresa holding little Samuel, and she looked rough. She had lost so much weight, and there were circles under her eyes. To be so low physically and to have Murph drinking as much as he did and not offering her the tenderness she needed—this dealt the final blow. Teresa's loss of blood had caused postpartum depression of the worst kind.

"I can't get that one night out of my mind," Teresa had told Edward. "I had the three older boys in the bathtub, and I was so weak that I just sat on the floor and leaned on the tub. I started to lose consciousness, so I crawled over to the window to call for Murph's help. He was reading his newspaper out on the back lawn. I heard him curse as he threw down his newspaper and began to stomp his way through the house and up the stairs. 'Can't I have one moment of peace?' He barked when he came into the bathroom. In that moment, I just wanted to jump out the window and run away and never come back.

I got to the phone and called his mother to come, then called the doctor. The doctor said, 'This is very bad. You need a prescription immediately. Have your husband get to the Pharmacy right away.' Well, wouldn't you know that Murph found a flat tire on our old car? The tire was always going flat. So instead of using the company car, which was against the rules, he decided to walk to the Pharmacy. It was over then for me. Remember when I said he had no problem using his company car for drinking binges in Cedarville? But was it ok to risk my life? It felt like an eternity waiting for him to come back that night."

Teresa had mentioned wanting to die. She had asked Murph to move out, and that was when Edward started crossing the line with her. He loved the Murphys and felt responsible for them. He loved them more than he had ever loved his own family. Edward visited Murph as well, feeling that he was doing his part for the whole family. Murph was in the depths of his drinking at that point and still living a large portion of the year up north in Modoc, while Teresa stayed in Delta City in their house near the church.

Edward was amazed that this went on for a couple of years in a chaste manner. Neither one of them planned to do something wrong. Teresa was gradually regaining her health and keeping in touch with Murph to see if he was making any progress. The reports weren't good. She was good friends with a lot of the ranchers near Alturas and their wives. Plus, the priest up there kept everyone informed. Murph was as low as he could get, and there had been talk about his visits to another man's wife.

Teresa always did everything by the book. She ate a healthy diet and tried to contribute to the church's various ministries. She did light exercises and had even gotten back to mowing the lawn. Edward had been mowing the lawn, but Teresa insisted on taking this chore back. She wanted Murph to see that she was ready to be a good helpmeet to him again. At night, when the children went to bed, Teresa explained that her one indulgence was to take a grilled cheese sandwich and the latest Time magazine to bed with her. She was trying to follow the psychiatrist's recommendations. He had explained that life was like a cross. "You need to balance your life with the four points of the cross—work, faith, play, and love."

"He told me I was low on play," Teresa had reported to Edward with a faraway look in her eyes.

Edward should have known better. He knew Teresa well enough by then to know that she would do everything the doctor recommended—to a T. She had also regained her composure and her position of command. Teresa had a devious streak, and there was no getting around it, but Edward still didn't believe she had planned their transgression. Either way, nothing would absolve him of his own sin, and wisdom was hard-won in this case.

Edward remembered stories of Teresa in her younger years. Like the time she had asked a young man to drive her for hours to attend a party back in her hometown in Idaho. When they pulled up to the party, Teresa thanked him for the ride and, to his chagrin, sent him on his way. The young man had called Teresa's parents and told them that their daughter was back in town at a party. Her parents drove to the party, unknowingly crossed paths with her, and later found her snug and fast asleep in bed back at their farm. "Actually, first I had accidentally crawled into bed with Gus, the old hunchback. Boy, my sisters never let me live that one down. You see, my parents had given him my old room. Here I thought they would be so happy to see me, but instead, they were just ready to see me move on in life." Teresa had laughed.

Then there was the story about her already being engaged to another man when she met Murph. "He had a weird last name, Shelleberger, and I couldn't imagine taking on that name. His mother loved me, of course, all their mothers loved me. Once I decided to marry Murph, I just took Shelleberger's ring off and pawned it." Another laugh.

Teresa was the type of woman young men were warned about. Yet, Edward saw the frailty beneath it all. It showed when she expressed that her parents weren't happy to see her. Or it showed when she felt responsible for her brother, J.B.'s, death. Edward forgave her for everything.

Edward would never claim that Teresa had planned it all, but there had been moments when he wasn't so sure. When he had first met the Murphys, with all their fine boys, Teresa had boasted about being a good Catholic wife and knowing how to do the "family planning." It was apparent then that Teresa loved to make men blush.

Edward never allowed himself to remember the incident in great detail. He had confessed it to the bishop and to God, and he never wanted to entertain those thoughts. It helped him in forgiving himself to remember the desperation in Teresa's voice when she had called his office that day. Murph had rejected her reconciliation attempts and had driven off for his season in the mountains. The older boys were in school, and Murph's mother had Samuel. Teresa had said that she wasn't sure that she could go on living and that her mood had sunk really low. She had asked Murph's mother to take Samuel so that maybe she could finally take a long, hot bath. Edward could tell that she had been drinking, which was not normal for her. He was worried about the combination of drinking, her depression medication, and a bath.

He rushed over, and that is when he would not allow any more thought to the incident. The bishop was very forgiving, considering the nature of the incident and his knowledge of Teresa and her situation. The church had even taken over the house payment for Teresa, and the parishioners had prayed that her marriage would be reconciled.

When Murph arrived in Modoc, there was a late snow, and it seemed providential that his work would have to be delayed. Teresa begged him to come back down and back home. The church was relieved. There was even more joy when the Murphys announced that they were expecting their fifth child. Edward hated to leave them, but he knew that he needed to get away. He begged to be transferred to Meadowbrook to oversee the new church. Designing churches was in his blood, after all. God's mercy and grace were showered upon him, and the transfer was accepted at the same time that Teresa's pregnancy was showing and before she kicked Murph out for the final time.

Edward might as well have been a celebrity the way Meadowbrook accepted him with open arms. They had been waiting years for their own resident pastor. The church, as well as the rectory, was set to be built, and Edward hit the ground running. Edward named the new church St. Michael's after his favorite intercessor, the Archangel Michael. Edward was so busy then, and a typical man, people might say, that it took him many months to connect the dots about the Murphys and all that had gone on.

Not even when he traveled down to have a drink with Murph, to celebrate the birth of his first daughter, did he realize something was amiss. He and Murph went together to see Teresa with the baby. Teresa had asked the court, in the divorce proceedings, that Murph never come unaccompanied to see her or the children. Murph was quite inebriated that morning, so he didn't notice all that transpired. This would be the first time Edward had seen Teresa since their indiscretion, and his heart ached with the same familial love for all of them.

"She's 99% Irish, my little Chrissy," Murph had boasted.

As Edward leaned in to take a look, Teresa had whispered, "Sorry to say, if she is Irish at all, it is from my side. I would say that she is 99% German." She looked up at Edward, "Wouldn't you say so, Edward?"

She had sent Edward's mind reeling, and he was thankful for the long drive back to Meadowbrook. He had a daughter? That beautiful baby girl was his own flesh and blood?

"I should leave the priesthood," Edward said out loud on the drive. But then what? He didn't think Teresa would actually want that. So different than after Samuel's birth,

Teresa looked quite strong holding Christine. Once again, she was in complete control of the situation.

All those years later, in the old Pontiac, Edward leafed through all the pictures of Christine that Teresa had sent him over the years. He found a picture of her first communion with Anthony on one side and Joseph on the other—both in their serving cassocks.

"Yes," Edward said out loud. "She is very German and in this one she looks very much like my dearest sister, Eleanor."

Teresa had written to say that Christine's stepfather, Patrick, had refused to attend her first communion. Edward didn't think that Teresa intended for him to feel guilty—she was sharing her thoughts, like, "Christine truly struck out in the father department. Of course, she still doesn't know about you. She never will, just like we agreed."

Edward removed his glasses and used a handkerchief to mop up all the tears. He spoke an oft-repeated prayer, "God, please be Christine's Father—that she would know you as an everywhere-presence in her life."

Chapter 24

On the one hand, Christine felt the weight of being one of the only ones alive who cared about Murph in his final days—on the other hand, she felt such peace in devoting herself to him. What could be more tragic than someone dying completely alone? She had slowly gotten to know Murph over the years, like when she took her kids down to meet him and to go to Disneyland. The first time Christine remembers laying eyes on him, long before Disneyland, was when she was in her early twenties and Murph picked her up to attend a funeral. He had asked her if she wanted a cigarette. She politely declined as she eyed that father of hers—a complete stranger.

Her brothers had largely moved on in life without Murph, and who could blame them? They were busy with families and successful careers. Anthony, always the angel, had come home from Vietnam to set up practice as a dermatologist in Delta City, living in the same vicinity as Murph. Anthony paid Murph occasional visits and handled all of his medical needs, but was far too busy with his practice, duties at the church, and his growing family, to do much more when Murph's health began to fail.

More than once, Christine had wondered why Teresa didn't decide to take care of him herself. She lived only minutes away in the same community, and they attended the same church. Life is so funny, Christine thought. She had heard of that happening often—former spouses coming back together to take care of each other in their golden years. That would have been such a nice full circle. But her mother was as independent as ever and would never admit that she was growing older.

So much had happened since Teresa and Murph had parted ways all those years ago, when Christine was a newborn. For starters, the "Patrick years" had happened. At the end of that marriage, before Patrick and Teresa had also parted ways, they had purchased a rural, waterfront property with just a tiny, primitive dwelling at Eagle Lake. Teresa fought for that property in the divorce. She had gone on to live many fulfilling years out there—the outdoorswoman in the high desert with her garden and Indian paintbrush flourishing amongst the sagebrush. She could fish, illegally, and skinny dip as often as she wanted. In the winter, she pulled her groceries in on a sled, and she cooked over a wood stove. Teresa was as happy as the eared grebes, a common sight on her lake.

Patrick, on the other hand, lived in the largest house in Alturas, perched on a tower of rock where the sights were endless. But the beautiful views, sunrises, and sunsets could do nothing for what Patrick found deep within himself. The glimpse into himself was too deep and too painful, and it pulled him away from all that was beautiful and good. Patrick must have felt that the only solution was to end his life, and so he did—a solitary ending to a solitary man living in a castle on a tower of rocks.

In the days and years that followed, Teresa would stare out at the lake for hours, and Christine and her siblings started to worry about their mother. More than once, Teresa said, "Maybe if I had stayed with Patrick, he would have found a reason to live," or she was even known to say, "Murph had said that he would drink himself to death without me. I meant my vows when I married him, and maybe I could have helped him recover—then he would have been a better dad to you kids." The younger kids would assure her, "It's ok, Mom, you wouldn't have had us if you had stayed with Murph. Why don't you move away from that lake, closer to us, and spend more time with your grandkids?"

Despite her occasional regrets, Teresa hated sympathy. The suggestion that she forgo her independence was enough for Teresa to regain control of her life, and so she joined the Peace Corps, as Joseph had. First, she traveled to Guatemala, but later spent the bulk of her time serving in Sierra Leone. Christine still couldn't believe that her mother managed that in her 60s, after raising eight children. "There is no one alive like my mother," Christine thought.

Christine had felt so sad about Patrick's death. During her adult years, she and Patrick would see each other at various occasions, usually centered around activities for her younger siblings and their families. A mutual respect had somehow developed between them. She had seen a look of admiration in his eyes more than once when she caught him looking at her.

It reminded Christine of the one time Patrick had shown admiration during her childhood.

Every year, Alturas hosted a fishing derby at Pine Creek Reservoir, and there was nothing Patrick liked more than fishing. He had invited Major General William F. Dean, the highest-ranking American officer held as a prisoner of war during the Korean War, to award prizes to the first-place girl and the first-place boy. Samuel loved to tell the story of how that day played out. "It was just you and me that day, Chrissy. You wore your little checked jacket. Patrick was annoyed that everyone else was busy and that you and I were his only prospects. Well, as luck would have it, as soon as the opening gunshot was fired, I spotted a shiny lure half buried in the dirt. They were against the rules, but I took my chances and tied it to my line. I immediately caught a huge trout. I ran around the reservoir and let you cast my line before I took my fish to the judges. Then you snagged one immediately, too! I told you to run it to the judges, and away you went, fish still hanging on the hook! We did it—we both won for the largest catch! Patrick was as pleased as punch when we got to pose for a picture with the Major General. You can even see him in the picture, looking so proud. Then he took us out for ice cream at Harold's afterward."

Poor Patrick, Christine thought. He couldn't seem to help the way he was. Before his death, Christine knew that Patrick had developed a fondness toward her husband, Pete, and their two children, Jacob and Kora Anne.

It had been so startling when they found a hasty note after his death that left a little money specifically for Christine and her children. Had she really been one of his last concerns? It was too heartbreaking to think about. Fatherhood can take many forms, and it was odd that both Murph and Patrick finished out their days patching together their own forms of fatherhood for Christine.

Murph had made it clear, up front, that he had made a bargain with God. He would give up drinking and smoking and give the rest of his life to God—including the bulk of his money from his inventions. Royalties from his toy sales were already set to go to a seminary on the East Coast. Christine was glad because she didn't want anyone to think she was helping him for money. She just felt sorry for him.

"What a lonely life he has lived," Christine thought sadly. He had missed raising his beautiful children—all so fun and intelligent. He certainly took great pride in talking about them— Francis was a renowned real estate developer in the area, Joseph had just been appointed a Superior Court Judge, Anthony was the head of Dermatology in a nearby hospital, Samuel ran a famous, historic hotel, and was also a beloved teacher. Then there was Christine, his charming, Irish daughter. She was a looker for sure, like her mother, and had given her own children a good, solid Catholic education—both Jacob and Kora Anne had even just been confirmed into the Catholic Church. Nothing could make Murph happier than that. Christine wondered if her poor father was not only making up for his own sins but also for his father's suicide in front of the altar in Illinois. "Poor Murph," She thought again.

Even as they got his affairs in order, there were no deep and healing conversations between Christine and her father— no apologies or mention of regrets. His intelligence and wit compensated for the lack of deep discussions. He loved trying to make Christine laugh and to see her beautiful smile. Christine tried several times to get her mother to come to Murph's house. "I just want my mom and dad in the same room for one time in my life," Christine thought. "Even if they bicker, I would love to see their humor come out—like the scenarios that Francis would recall from his boyhood."

In the end, Teresa only agreed to come to the hospital after Murph had lost his spark and speech with his final stroke. Christine hoped to see the compassionate side of her mother. "Well, here they are at last," Christine had thought, "I'm fifty years old and finally seeing my parents together, inside the same four walls. Yet there are unseen walls between them that are just as high. Murph is too far gone, but how hard would it be for my mother to say something kind to him? Give him peace at last? It is all so tragic. I never want to live that way. I want to be honest with my kids and apologize for my shortcomings."

They sat there for a while, and then Teresa broke the silence, "I don't know why you put so much energy into him. He wasn't a good father."

Christine fingered the ends of her sleeves a moment before responding, "Please don't say anything negative—he can probably hear you. Didn't you always tell me that it is better to give than to receive? I actually feel good inside knowing I gave him a little companionship at the end. It was easy to see that he loved me, even if he wasn't there for me earlier in life. Do you think I resemble him?"

Teresa let out a loud laugh, "Not in the least. No, your coloring and looks did not come from him."

Christine felt saddened by her mom's comment and decided just to pray silently. She gently enclosed Murph's hand in hers and began to repeat this prayer silently, "God have mercy on me, a sinner, God have mercy on my dad, a sinner…"

As they watched Murph's life slip away, Teresa commented, "I hope all that money he gave to the church is enough to get him through the pearly gates."

"Oh, Mom, you don't mean that," Christine exclaimed. "You shouldn't say such things. Pray for him."

"You know I will," Teresa responded, with a hint of sadness on her face. "Now I think I am about ready to go have a Bloody Mary for Old Murph's sake."

Chapter 25

As the years went by, Edward felt that God had blessed him with a real family at both the church and in the little house out back. It's a blessing to grow old with someone, and when Edward finally woke up, he realized he was growing old with Alice. Edward and Alice still watched the sunrise together after he fed the cats. She would hand him his coffee while she hid behind him in her robe and curlers. They didn't have long, deep conversations, but there was comfort in repeating the same little phrases, like Alice asking, "Do you need me to remind you about what is on your calendar?" Or Edward asking, "How is Buddy getting along?" Either one might question the other, "Did you remember to take your medication?"

After Alice's mother died, Bonnie became her closest friend. She often joined Alice and Edward for dinner in the rectory. "Bless her heart," Bonnie would say, "Mrs. Pedigraw knows how much we all love her Shepherd's Pie and she loves feeding the shepherd of our flock." Mrs. Pedigraw often delivered dinners, especially after her husband passed. Occasionally, she even dined with them, saying things like, "Have you noticed how often the women are bringing those boxed, instant pasta salads to the parish suppers lately? They give me indigestion. How hard is it to cook noodles, chop up some vegetables and cheese, and add a little salad dressing? I am not sure what those mothers do with all their time—maybe they watch soap operas. Oh well, I don't mind cooking extra to bring—what else am I going to do with my time?"

"Bless your heart," Bonnie would reply.

Matthew had avoided Edward in the first few weeks after Andrew's failed healing at Dochero, all those years ago. It's not that Matthew was rude—he just seemed introspective and maybe like he was dealing with his own demons. Edward would catch glimpses of him in the back alley or as he walked to the church's side door. Edward lifted a hand, but Matthew just ducked his head and continued on.

The family thankfully kept attending church, and Edward was pleased to see more people showing warmth toward them. Edward noticed that Matthew had the same childlike, expectant look as his son during Edward's homilies. "Please God, get through to him," Edward would pray.

It took Edward those first few weeks to get his plan together and put it into action. He had decided to leave his wooden box of pictures and letters hidden out by the aspen trees. He had found an old oak tree with a huge knot at the base of its trunk and a hidden hole beneath. He wrapped the box in plastic and tucked it inside. This way, he could enjoy a drive and go look through his things without having to go by the bank first. Then, when he died, no one would find it. It was his treasure and his alone. Edward was glad to do away with the safety deposit box altogether. Being outside, searching for his hidden treasure, made him feel like a kid again, and he went weekly at first.

It was one of Teresa's letters to him that helped him form his plan. Edward felt a renewed sense of gratitude for how everything turned out between him and Teresa. It had turned into a solid friendship, and that was perfect. It could never have been a marriage—he didn't believe in Hollywood-type love affairs. With all the couples he had counseled and the confessions he had heard, it was easy to see that the world's ideas of romance did not exist—at least, not for long. It was the enemy's ploy to get people constantly seeking after that sort of thing.

Edward didn't hold onto any illusions about Teresa caring for him in that way. It sadly seemed that Teresa never learned that lesson, the lesson of self-sacrifice toward a man or toward either of her husbands, to be more specific. It was all very sad to hear of Murph living out his days alone and of her second husband's suicide. Could it have been different for either of them if Teresa had stood by their side in some sort of companionship, at least? That really is what she had offered Edward—more than she had offered either of them. She had been a true friend to him, despite both of their faults. Edward prayed for God to remember both Murph and Patrick in His kingdom.

Edward and Teresa shared a mutual heartache—the heartache of not being able to raise their daughter together— their precious, beautiful daughter, Christine. Nothing had driven Edward to trust God more than to trust Him completely with Christine. That God would really step in and physically and emotionally meet her needs.

Sometimes, when Edward would pray for her, he would also repeat this line to himself—"God is wherever you let God in." Then he would say, "Please, God, I pray that Christine would let you in." After the Vietnam War, it was tragic to see just how many children didn't have fathers. And if their fathers came home, there was often even more damage inflicted because of the trauma the soldiers had endured. There were so many children out there who lacked real fathers, and the only solution was the Heavenly Father. Could his prayers for Christine make up for everything else? Edward had no choice but to believe that.

And he had that one, precious memory from so many years ago. Edward could still see the look on Christine's face, hear the sound of her voice, and then feel her hand in his after she asked, "Father Edward? I would like to hold your hand. May I?"

Teresa had vowed never to tell Christine who her real father was.

"I know pride isn't good, Edward, but I must keep my pride in this area. What kind of example would I be setting for her and the other children if they knew what had happened? And I have been the victim of ridicule and shame many times in my life, for being Catholic, too. Back in Idaho, the bus used to drop all the Catholics blocks away from our school, even in the wet and cold weather, and then drive right by the Catholic School as they took the rest of the kids to the public high school. They easily could have taken us all the way. Remember, I told you the kids would yell out the bus windows and call us Cat-Lickers? I will not have Christine suffer knowing that the Catholic Church had deprived her of a father."

Edward didn't entirely agree with Teresa, but he knew he was stuck in a hard place. He considered leaving the church, but something told him that Teresa wasn't really interested in making a life with him. Edward had moments of deep regret—wondering if he had done the right thing. It was in those times that he would inadvertently draw blood with the arrowhead and then turn to prayer and prostrations. And a life quickly passed in this way.

The letter that caught his attention was about Teresa needing money. "Bless her heart that she never did blackmail me," Edward thought. "I wouldn't put blackmail past her, but she only did those types of things toward people who had greatly wronged her. Like when her sisters teased and threatened to tell on her when they heard that Teresa had accidentally crawled into bed with their old hunchbacked farmhand, Gus." Edward chuckled. "Imagine how terrified Teresa had been when she realized it! Teresa had to bribe her sisters into silence with her hard-earned money."

Edward again thought back to the church, and no need for any blackmail. "Thankfully, the church was so good to us." After their sin, they both immediately confessed to the bishop. The bishop followed protocol exactly and never breathed a word to anyone outside of that circle. He showered them both with the grace and mercy of God and had shown great compassion for the circumstances that led them to that place. Some gossipers had certainly put two and two together, and that must be how his family back home eventually heard the news. Edward could only pray that they would recognize the common thread of human frailty and their own need for God.

The bishop had approved Edward's transfer to Meadowbrook with complete confidence that Edward desired to help a church in need. He sent Edward with his blessing, and that was all Edward needed.

The Holy Family Catholic Church took over the mortgage of the sweet little house Teresa shared with her children—its front door framed by climbing roses. They wanted to ease Teresa's stress and prayed she would reconcile her marriage. It was with great sadness that the attempt failed, but the church wanted to continue providing a stable environment for the beloved family.

Edward was glad that Teresa felt she could be real with him. She never pretended to be a saint, and Edward knew that, with her returned vitality, she would be the stellar mom she had already proven herself to be. Even after she moved permanently to the mountains, Edward trusted she would be better than any Girl Scout Leader for her kids, or any Boy Scout Leader, for that matter. And she would do it all, with a whistle and a smile.

Edward smiled despite himself. Yes, he was still entertained by Teresa. Even when she could be a little cruel at times, he knew she didn't really mean it. The letter at the time said that her new husband, Patrick, had fooled her into thinking he would treat all the kids equally. "It's like he somehow knows, Edward. Somehow, Patrick seems to know that Christine is different from the boys. Maybe he is just jealous that she and I are so close, but sometimes I get the feeling that he suspects something. He is pretty bright, after all, and has done enough sneaking around in his life that now he suspects everyone else of doing the same. What is it called? Oh yes, blame-shifting or deflection.

Twice now, he has accepted horses from clients in trade for his legal work. One was a black-and-white packhorse named Prince, and the other was an old strawberry roan saddle horse named Blue John. He acted like they were big presents for Christine, but only let her ride them one time each before he gave them back. Anyway, I'm not trying to make you feel bad, but it makes me feel better to write it all out.

I was wondering if you could send some occasional money for Christine's wardrobe? I can't have the boys looking sharp and then her looking drab. It makes me think back to her baby shower. Do you remember how she received no less than sixty dresses as a newborn? You know how vain I am—I don't hide it. That sure made me happy to see our baby girl showered in such finery. You have been so good to send money over the years. Not enough to make me go all fat and lazy, haha, but just enough to be a blessing. I appreciate it more than I could ever say. It's just that now that Christine is growing, clothes are more expensive. I also want her to have a good wardrobe before she heads off to Mt. St. Paul's next August. That was such a good recommendation, and thank you for your promise to help when the time comes.

Edward, have you ever realized how much of a blessing you are to others? One of the saddest things has been taking the boys away from you. They love you so much and still talk about you. Anthony especially gets starry-eyed whenever he says your name. Sometimes I wonder if he will want to be a priest. Anyway, what is on my mind is that you are surely blessing the people around you even now. You have the power to change people's lives every day. I have already been praying for you, and now I pray that you will realize the power of Christ in you. Well, goodbye for now. Patrick will be home soon and will want his first bourbon while he makes his green salad with anchovies. He really isn't as bad as I let on. I will try to make a go of it, I promise. Love always, Teresa."

Then she had added, "P.S., Did Murph tell you about his new game? It seems to be a hit with the kids, and I am happy for him. His sister-in-law, Betty, let me know. She also said that her husband, Bill, has just been promoted to Chief of

Orthopedics at the hospital in Delta City. It makes me happy that my children have all inherited good genes."

"That's right," Edward thought, "Dr. Bill! I had forgotten about him. I wonder if he could…?"

This was how God worked through Teresa, even through an old letter, to give Edward an idea. It was like a floodgate had been opened or like he had suddenly won the lottery. Edward had never been so instantly happy—nearly giddy.

He quickly stuffed the box back into the knot of the tree and sped back down into the valley. He made appointments and began to get his affairs in order. "God is wherever you let God in," Edward thought. "And that even means letting him into your bank account."

Chapter 26

It didn't take much for Christine to take a wider look at her life. Life is often very comical, and Christine loved to laugh.

When her kids, now known as Jake and Kora, started middle school, she took a job as a diet counselor. It wasn't fair, really—not for the patients. Christine could eat a whole pizza by herself and never put on a pound. Not to say that she didn't work at it, as her mother had taught her. Most days, she would do her Jane Fonda workouts in the evenings.

After that job, Kora was mortified when Christine took a job at a local Kiwi Factory as a production line supervisor.

When Christine picked Kora up from school, wearing her hiking boots, Kora said, "Please, I don't want my friends to know that you work there. Can't our family just be normal?"

Christine enjoyed all of her unique jobs and, before she knew it, she wasn't shy anymore—especially after taking a Dale Carnegie Public Speaking course. After a time working as a realtor, she set her eyes on her biggest goal yet, to be a Tour Director for one of the world's most prestigious tour companies. She landed the job just when she was empty-nesting, and she never felt more at home than wowing her clients with charm and knowledge from the front of a tour bus—New England's fall colors whizzing by the windows and embellishing her every word. "My life is a dream," she would often exclaim to herself. "I never want to stop exploring the world."

A once-in-a-lifetime experience was offered to her during those touring years—Christine was chosen as one of four interns to work with scientists at Mesa Verde National Park as part of the Save America's Treasures grant program. While Christine spent her days in the cliff dwellings of the Ancestral Pueblo people, the Anasazi, she truly felt like her mother's daughter, full of respect for the people who lived so closely to nature and who persevered through countless trials. Christine never felt more alive than during her adventures— summiting Mt. Shasta, backpacking through the Trinity Alps, and camping each summer with her brothers and sisters and all their children in Modoc County—so like their days at Deep Creek.

"Was it caught or taught—this zeal for life?" Christine had asked Teresa during one of her visits after Murph's death.

"I think both, and I'll take all the credit," Teresa responded. "Your father's family didn't know how to have fun unless it hit them in the head. You also got your attractive ankles from me, by the way. The only thing I'll give your father credit for is your tendency to be so introspective. I have been told it is a good thing. So you are balanced—a lot of fun but also introspective at times. That is probably why you are such a good listener. That Kora Kar Kid must have gotten all that introspection from you. She makes me uncomfortable since she became a Protestant. I am always afraid she is going to preach to me. No one can actually be that happy. I prefer Jake, he is more balanced—and with such good humor!"

"Mom, you aren't supposed to play favorites with your grandchildren, and Kora is actually that happy. That is her gift, I guess. Plus, giving someone a nickname, like Kora Kar Kid, is a sure sign of affection."

"Well, anyway, it is time for a martini." Teresa rose from the couch and went over to her minibar. As she prepared the drink, her back to Christine, she said, "Did I already mention that Father Edward died since your last visit?"

It had been so long since Christine heard that name that it took her a minute to recall the connection. "Oh, yes, Father Edward. I am sorry to hear that, Mom. Do you think he had heard of Murph's passing, and if they had stayed in touch?"

"Probably," Teresa said, turning back to her with a martini in hand. "Would you like one?"

Christine nodded and reached out for the drink.

"Did you know that Francis has been recording my life story?" Teresa asked. "This made me think of it because we always have our martini after the day's recording. He has to maintain his favorite son status after all!" She chuckled. "Well, anyway, all that time talking with Francis, and the introspection, as you could call it, has made me think so much about all of you kids. I have decided that you had it tougher than all of my kids—you were sandwiched in the middle and never had a father figure."

"It's ok, Mom. I have really had the best life. You don't need to feel bad about it."

"Well, it's just that I do, and I have decided that I want to treat you—I want to take you to travel the world during the years that I have left. What do you think?"

Christine tripped over her words at first, "Wow, well, I don't know what to say. I don't have the money for that right now, and it sounds costly."

"It will be expensive because I want to go first class on everything, and I will pay for it. I really want to see part of the Iditarod route and take you on a dogsled ride there. You know I have my favorite dog sled team! I want to take you places because you are my miracle, after all, and I want you to know just how very loved you are."

"That is so dear, Mom, and I love you, too. I'm still just wondering how you can afford it? You would be on the streets without Francis and the others helping you financially."

"You know that I have my ways. It's fashion show money!" Teresa winked at Christine and laughed. "Don't look a gift horse in the mouth, Chrissy. We are going and that's that. When can you leave? I am thinking a cruise to Alaska and then that dog sled ride while we are there."

"I'm not sure," Christine said slowly, thinking. "I know I need to get my eyes checked next week—I'm taking every precaution, but they say my macular degeneration is slightly worse. Did anyone in our family have macular degeneration? I haven't heard of it in our family before, and it looks like I will need a new prescription soon." Christine pushed her glasses up her nose. "But I suppose I could be ready in a couple of weeks. Wow, I still can't believe this—thank you, Mom!"

Christine stood up and grabbed Teresa by the hands, twirling her in a circle. As if on cue, they both burst out in an old Girl Scout song, "He's got the whole world in His hands, He's got the whole world in His hands, He's got the whole wide world in His hands, He's got the whole world in His hands!"

Later that evening, they lay together on the guest bed, reminiscing about Joseph and Patrick Jr., both of whom had passed away in the last few years. It was almost too heartbreaking to say their names out loud, but gradually the memories would bring them smiles.

"Do you remember when Joseph brought Yogi home? Also, I'll never stop hearing Patrick's little voice when he would say, 'That's just a 'neaky old cop.'"

"We laughed so much, didn't we, Mom?"

"Oh, we did. And all those camping trips and skinny dipping at the creek or the lake. I bet you could still hear our laughter there, over the waters. All of you kids have a sense of humor and are so adventurous and smart." Then she added, "I know I have made some mistakes through the years, and I am sorry."

"I am not sure what you mean. We have had a great life," Christine said. "Besides, the words you like to recite from Stephen Cosgrove's poem still ring true—'Mistakes are always mistakes, or so I've heard them say, but if it teaches a lesson, the mistake will go away!'"

They giggled again and then lay in silence for a moment before Teresa jumped up and said, "Well, I guess it's time to go to bed. Tomorrow will be busy for me with all the trip planning. Don't forget to say your prayers, Chrissy." Teresa hugged Christine.

"Mom? Speaking of Kora and her newfound Protestantism, I was wondering if you have ever, as she puts it, 'accepted Jesus as your Savior?'"

"That's the thing, Chrissy, I am not sure where the Protestants come up with this stuff. Reassure her that Christ is my salvation—our salvation—and Jesus is the fountain of life. Let her think about those words—they are much more traditional than the things she says."

"Ok, those words are beautiful, what you just said, and also, Mom, before you go? I was looking up at the crucifix on the wall. You used to hang it in my room. Who gave it to you?"

"Oh, that. It's actually yours." Teresa gave a nervous laugh. "I kept meaning to give it to you, but it has been a comfort to me over the years. You can take it now if you'd like."

"I wouldn't do that to you. I would hate to think of you being lonely without it. Maybe just put a piece of tape on the back with my name for when you are gone—so the others don't snatch it." Christine clasped her hand over her mouth. "Wait, never mind. I don't like to talk like that. I'm sorry."

Teresa laughed, "That's true, you better take it back." She gave Christine a playful pinch on her cheek. "We have too many places to go before you all start dividing up my things— before my body is even cold." She laughed again.

As Teresa walked out, she turned back, "You had asked where it came from, the crucifix—Father Edward gave it to you on the day you were born. Several priests came with Murph that day to have a drink and celebrate. Father Edward had a note with it that I memorized, which said, 'Welcome to the world, Christine. There isn't a girl alive who could have a more beautiful mother, a more proud dad, or four big brothers who are more enamored with their baby sister than you. I am gifting you this crucifix, and I will ask your mother to hang it in every room where you ever lay your pretty little head. That way you will know that you are never alone, 'For He shall give His angels charge over you. To keep you in all your ways. In

240

their hands they shall bear you up, lest you dash your foot against a stone.'"

"That is the sweetest thing I have ever heard," Christine said with a sigh. It was odd, just then, how that memory immediately popped up, the day she had met Father Edward to talk about Georgia's death, and when she had taken his hand after first refusing it, "I am so glad I took his hand, after all." Christine thought. Then she suggested to her mom, "Maybe having that crucifix in my room back in Alturas was why I never felt alone?"

"Maybe so. Good night, Daughter." Teresa walked down the hallway, and Christine couldn't help but get up and follow her at a distance. She watched from around the corner as her mom knelt beside her bed, with the soft glow of the light around her head, and then recited her prayer list.

"Or, maybe this is why I have never felt alone," Christine thought.

Chapter 27

"Life is beautiful," Edward thought. "The beauty gets me at every turn these days, it seems." Once again, Edward wiped the tears from beneath his glasses. This wasn't necessarily the kind of beauty that is seen with the eyes.

Other, less desirable, things had "gotten" Edward, too—like throat cancer and becoming more blind with each passing day. The church had allowed him to convalesce in the rectory, as the new priest was happy to share. The new priest, Father Bud, Alice's son, had become like a son to Edward. All those years ago, when Edward finally called him, he found that Buddy was a joy to talk to. They talked about baseball, the Bible, Billy Sunday, and the meaning of "vocation." Edward had been the first to explain to Buddy that "in Latin, 'vocatio' could mean 'a call' or 'summons.'" After several conversations, he had asked Buddy directly, "Your mother has indicated that you might have heard the call to the priesthood?"

Buddy answered, "I think I have. It didn't come through anything notable or miraculous. It seems to be coming from the fact that no job seems to fit. I know I am not lazy— it's just that contentment with a job has eluded me so far. And then I had a failed engagement. I seem to do better alone in that department. All the while, I keep feeling drawn to church and to God's Word. I have a desire to study it and the history of the Catholic Church. It's almost like I am being called by default."

"That can be ok," Edward reassured him. "Look at Jonah, he didn't exactly follow a yellow brick road leading to ministry. I did, comparatively. Except that the true summons of my heart only came about quite recently, not when I first went to seminary."

"That is interesting. I hope you will tell me more about that." Buddy said, and then added, "I was hoping I could talk to you about seminaries. It's funny because I have never felt scholarly, but now it's all looking so attractive to me. I'm wondering how one affords seminary. They are so expensive, and my mom and I have no savings."

"It's funny you should bring that up, but let me reassure you, if a plan is from the Lord, He will make a way. Let's plan on talking weekly and see what transpires. Maybe you can come and listen to baseball games on the radio with me? We can also pray together."

Edward had already decided to pay Buddy's way through seminary, but he knew better than to rush it. Besides the significant change he made to his will, Edward had also put aside a considerable amount to take Andrew to see Dr. Bill in Delta City.

It wasn't easy to convince Matthew at first. He had a mistrust of doctors after so many had coldly asked for large amounts of money with no assurance that anything would help Andrew. He had finally agreed to let Edward help after Edward and Anne had a conversation behind the rectory one evening. It was a warm spring evening, and the lilac had just bloomed. Edward had forgotten his glasses again. They didn't really help much anyway, and, for all he knew, he was alone back there.

He had pressed his face against the cool, fragrant blossoms and had lost himself in the moment.

A voice broke his reverie.

"What did you say?"

It was funny the resemblance between Margaret and Anne—the way they could appear from nowhere and demand an answer.

"Oh, did I say something? I do talk to myself more often than I want to admit," Edward replied.

"Yes, you do," Anne offered. "This time I specifically heard you say, 'I don't think anything could smell more heavenly than this.'"

"Well, that is true. I do think Heaven might smell like a lilac," Edward said with a sigh.

"It is interesting because those are the exact words that I heard Christine, that girl from Mt. St. Paul's, say so many years ago," Anne said.

"What do you mean? Where was she?" Edward asked.

"She was right there, in that same spot where you are, doing the same thing, sticking her face into the blossoms. And then she said those same words."

"That is something, for sure." Edward said, and then, softly, as a prayer, "Thank you, God."

"I already knew that God was in this, somehow," Anne continued. "It's been as plain as day. Because there was another time, too, you know, years later. One day, I needed to get out of the house when I was pregnant with Margaret. I took a walk to your "Dochero"—and she was there again—Christine. This time she had her husband with her, and he was taking pictures of her on the bridge."

"Isn't that something?" Edward said. "What did she look like?"

"She was gorgeous, of course, just like when she was in school here. Her hair was dark, with curls framing her face. Her skin was beautiful and pale, not a freckle to speak of. People like her used to make me sick—she was still as skinny as a schoolgirl. She was pressing her face into the roses next to the bridge, and you could tell that her husband just adored her."

"Did they say anything?" Edward asked, trying to imagine the scene.

"Yes, her husband said he had never seen a prettier picture. Christine replied, shyly, that it was just the effect of 'Dochero—this is my happy place on earth.'"

"I am sorry it was so annoying to you," Edward sympathized. Then to himself, Edward thought, "Christine was so close—I could have seen her. But I guess Anne needed to see her more than me."

Anne continued, "It's fine. God obviously had His reasons for all of this, even for that day. It's impossible that it was all just chance—all the times I saw her and noticed her. Then just now, with you and the lilac. I have decided that you will still be the one to help Andrew, even if he wasn't healed at 'Dochero'. Do you know what did happen there, Father Edward?" Anne asked.

"No, what?" Edward was annoyed with his failing eyesight. He wished he could see her face more clearly. He had to rely on just listening.

"I think it was Matthew who was healed that day—our family actually. All those things that Andrew said down by the creek. Matthew didn't show it, but I know he finally let his guard down. Thank you."

"Don't thank me. Let's just thank the Lord," Edward replied.

"I am going to talk Matthew into letting you take us to Delta City. There is just one condition—would you let Matthew drive us all in your car? That is one of his dreams, to drive that Old Pontiac."

"That is a fabulous idea and probably a safer one, too. As bad as my eyesight is."

So there were many small miracles in those days. Not the kinds of miracles that are known to large crowds. Just things like Buddy regularly listening to baseball games with Edward, and with Bonnie, Alice, and Mrs. Pedigraw chatting in the kitchen. When Matthew drove the Pontiac, he and Andrew wore matching grins. Soon after, Edward decided to sign the pink slip over to Matthew's name. These were the kinds of small miracles that Anne, Edward, and Alice treasured up in their own hearts. They knew the power of God in the way things unfolded.

One of the things that Edward treasured most of all was their bustling soup kitchen at St. Clement's. Nothing in life made him feel as useful as regularly feeding the poor. "Yes, the 'poor will always be with us.' We might as well stop complaining and just keep feeding them—this is our salvation," Edward philosophized.

One day, as his cancer was getting to be unbearable, Edward had borrowed the car from a reluctant Matthew and traveled out to his spot, practically just feeling his way on the road, since he could barely see, and he pulled out the box for the last time. He really shouldn't have been driving, but the road was most often empty of other travelers. He unfolded one of his favorite notes from Teresa and held it very close to make out the words.

She had just celebrated a birthday, and Christine and the kids had gifted her with a Bleuet camp stove. Teresa had seen "how well Jake's stove had worked in a downpour, and I am tickled pink about mine!" She also mentioned that they had all been together for Jake and Kora's confirmation into the Catholic Church in Chico. "Kora is kind of an annoying little thing, but I call her my little Kora Kar Kid," Teresa explained again. "When she was little, she was only happy when she was in her little ladybug car. Poor Chrissy had to lug that ladybug everywhere she went. There wasn't room for anything else in her trunk but that huge ladybug. But she did it, and you would be pleased to see what a good mother Chrissy is to those kids. Now that Kora is older, she is always happy, no ladybug car needed. Anyway, I drove up for the kids' confirmation. It was so funny that Bishop James was the one to confirm them. Do you think he knew that they were your grandchildren?"

Edward wiped his tears and his nose again. He thought again to himself, "Of course, Bishop James knew. He had been so faithful to keep track of Edward's family over the years, with zero judgment, only with love and a concern that they would be blessed by God. Teresa had also written to Edward a lot about her grandson, Jake. Their grandson. It was easy to see that Teresa adored Jake. "He is brilliant," she had reported more than once. "Just you wait, Jake will go on to build and invent things. He is very handsome, too. Maybe he takes after your side more than I would easily admit."

"Please, God, bless them," Edward said for the millionth time. "Please bless Christine and her children and their children, to a thousand generations." The tears were really falling then. "Forgive me, Lord, for my sins against you. Please don't hold them against them. And, one day, when I am gone, would you please show Christine the world? That she and Teresa could travel together and finally ride on a dogsled? Teresa is still the most adventurous woman I know, and it seems like Christine is following suit. My little world has been narrow, in that way, but that has been ok for me. I have loved serving you, Lord, and serving the flock here and at the other churches. I pray that I can serve for many days to come.

Lord, Bishop James once told me that one's life for you, and the way you work in a person, could be called their 'liturgy.' May it be so. May my liturgy include helping Buddy and Andrew and his family, and, one day, when I am gone, may it include showing Christine more of this beautiful world that you have created. Show her kids the world, too. Give them all an endless capacity for your beauty and for your creation, and give them a desire to serve you.

If there is even one small thing I have done in this life worthy of your kingdom, Lord, please use it. Please give Christine her liturgy—her life with you and for you."

Epilogue

"What you long for will be given you; what you love will be yours forever." Pope Leo I

"This is exactly the spot where I would kneel in the morning with the nuns," Christine said as she knelt in the little chapel at Mt. St. Paul's, the sun shining down on her head through the stained-glass windows.

"You are still as agile as a schoolgirl, Mom!" Kora exclaimed. "Not many people your age could get up and down like that—let alone kneel on that hard floor."

"I feel like a schoolgirl again, and I can remember everything as clearly as if it were yesterday."

Kora and her daughter, Sally, were touring Christine's old boarding school, and Christine had taken them to the chapel. Kora and Sally were caught up in the excitement of imagining it all—a whole year spent at the charming boarding school amongst the towering incense cedars of the region.

One highlight was visiting the old mining museum and taking photos by the relics and on the whimsical bridge over the creek. As they stood on the bridge looking down, Christine said, "We called it 'Dochero.'"

"What is a 'Dochero'?" Kora asked.

"It is just a word—we made it up."

It had been an exciting year of discovery for them, starting with a pop-up ad that caught Kora's attention before Christmas. When Christine opened the Ancestry kit on Christmas morning, Kora said, "Maybe we will find out more about your Irish heritage."

"Murph always said I was 99% Irish," a fact that Christine had always been proud of. Her trip to Ireland was one of the highlights of her life. When her results came back, Christine called and asked if Kora would come over and interpret them with her.

They sat together in front of the screen that evening as they both tried to figure out what everything meant—never once expecting any significant surprises.

"I recognize a lot of the names on my mom's side, but how come I don't know these names on the paternal side? And it says 0% Irish on the paternal side." Christine remarked.

They looked at each other and realized in that exact moment what it all meant—instead of Irish, they were very German in heritage, and Christine's "father" wasn't her father after all. To them, the discovery spelled "Adventure," and it was a gift from God.

It was initially challenging to connect the DNA results to Christine's biological father. Finally, on St. Patrick's Day, Christine and Kora decided to get down to business. "Let's ask St. Patrick to pray for us first," Christine had said.

With paper and notes in hand, they weren't going to give up until they discovered something. Kora clicked on a census record that had gone unnoticed due to a misspelling. This record showed another male in Christine's suspected family in Ohio. This newly discovered male was named Edward. Edward was not present in the other census records because of the time period. When Kora clicked on Edward's draft card, it was as if trumpets sounded—it gave the address of Christine's family's church, three and a half blocks away from their home address, and the dates were just months from her birth year. And sure enough, Edward's emergency contact was a bishop.

"It was Father Edward," Christine whispered. "My dad was a priest."

The miraculous gift kept giving, and later that day, they found a photo of Edward online. Kora remarked, "Look! He has that same bashful expression I have seen on you at that age!"

This discovery revealed something that Christine and Kora had always felt but couldn't pinpoint—the thought that they felt "blessed." On the first trip to Pine Valley, Kora pondered out loud, "Of course, everyone has the potential to be blessed, but do they count the blessings? Do they look for them? Do they thank God for them? Is a blessing even a blessing if it isn't acknowledged?"

Christine replied, "That's true. I have always felt blessed. My parents might have sinned, but who is without sin?"

During their time in Pine Valley, they took flowers to Edward's neglected grave in the Catholic Cemetery. Then later, after going to the mining museum, they visited the cemetery across the street from both St. Clement's and Mt. St. Paul's. They saw a man mowing the lawn and assumed he was old enough to have known Father Edward. He at first didn't notice their attempts to get his attention, and they almost gave up. Finally, Kora, demonstrating some of her Grandma Teresa's grit, gave one last dramatic attempt to wave him down, and it worked.

"Yes, he wore dark-rimmed glasses and was a man of mystery. He was well-liked." The man said, after they asked if he knew Father Edward.

"He was my father," Christine told him.

The man answered, "Yes, I saw the resemblance between you two immediately."

They all stood in silence for a moment, as if in shock.

"Could you tell us any more about him?" Sally finally asked.

"Yes, I knew him quite well. I was born with an infirmity. Meeting Father Edward was quite interesting at first." The man chuckled. "He took me to this place that he called 'Dochero' and baptized me in the creek. My parents had hoped I would be healed there."

"Really?" Kora exclaimed. "He really called it Dochero? How is that possible?"

"It is a miracle," the man replied. "My mother had seen you down there, too, Christine, calling it Dochero. Anyway, much later, Father Edward paid for me to see an Orthopedic Surgeon in Delta City, and I was healed, after all."

Christine hugged herself then, as if chilled by this revelation.

254

As they walked back to the car, Kora asked, "What did he say his name was again?"

Christine and Sally answered together, "Andrew."

On the drive home from Pine Valley, they discussed their discoveries.

Christine said, "I think the biggest treasure is the copy of the eulogy given by Bishop James. He remarked that at least 65 priests were in attendance at my dad's funeral. He also said that when they asked Father Edward if he possessed any ecclesiastical dignities, Father Edward replied that he had none. I wonder what ecclesiastical dignitaries are?"

Kora replied, "I am not sure, but either way, he sounded very humble."

"I love what this couple said—they knew Father Edward for decades," Christine continued. "They said he was 'kind, gentle, understanding but firm in teaching the truths of the Faith.' But I think my very favorite part is the poem that Bishop James read at the end." Christine read it out loud.

> "'To live in the midst of the world,
> Without wishing its pleasure;
> To be a member of each family,
> Yet belonging to none;
> To share all sufferings;
> To penetrate all secrets;
> To heal all wounds;
> To go from people to God,
> And offer Him in their prayers;
> To return from God to the people;
> To bring pardon and hope.
> My God, what a life, and it is yours,
> O priest of Jesus Christ.'"

After sitting in silence for a while, Kora said, "I am so glad that Uncle Francis recorded Grandma Teresa's life story. There is so much good stuff in those CDs! As I listened, I realized that our family has a legacy of prayer. That is such a gift. I especially like the story of Great Grandma Theodora by her washing tub."

Kora continued to tell the story, "One of Grandma Teresa's most poignant memories was when she was very young, standing by her mother, Theodora, at the washing tub on the banks of Little Goose Creek in Wyoming. As was normal, they heard the noon bell ring from town. On that particular day, however, Teresa saw her mother put her face in her apron to pray. For decades, she wondered why 'Mother didn't always pray when the bell rang?'

Many years later, while pregnant with Anthony, Grandma asked her mother why she had prayed that day when the bell rang. 'Oh, that is because the bell that day meant that World War I had finally ended.' Her mother responded. See? That is just one example of our rich heritage of prayer."

"I love that," Christine responded, with a faraway look in her eye.

Sally piped up, "When I get home, I want to research where the word 'Dochero' might have come from."

"I made it up," Christine said again.

A year later, discoveries continued. It was true that 'Dochero' could not be found on an internet search. But one morning, Kora called Christine and excitedly shared two things she had stumbled upon in her Orthodox Christian readings.

"This part is amazing—an author shared the traditional Orthodox belief that a priest's descendants will be blessed for many generations. Isn't that great?" Kora asked before continuing, "We know having a Catholic priest as an ancestor is not quite the same thing, but, then again, is it? We are all in need of God's mercy."

"What could be better?" Christine asked.

"Just wait until you hear this part from my devotional. It mentioned a monastery on Mt. Athos, Greece—Dochiariou. I'll text you the spelling because it is so close to Dochero. Mt. Athos is known as the Garden of the Theotokos, the Mother of God. Tradition tells that Mary, the Mother of God, shipwrecked off the coast of the island while sailing with St. John to Cyprus. She asked her Son to make it her garden. Mt. Athos is regarded as a sacred place where pilgrims, having left aside their worldly cares, find peace and, occasionally, miracles. I also saw in the news that Mel Gibson recently visited Mt. Athos and said it was the most sacred place he has ever been. Have you heard of Mt. Athos's Dochiariou?"

"No, I have never heard of it," Christine replied, "but it sounds like another miracle!"

"Yes!" Kora exclaimed. "And then I couldn't believe what Edmund said the other day about your confirmation name."

"Remind me again?" Christine asked. "There has just been so much."

"He said he asked you how you got your confirmation name, Margaret. You said Grandma Teresa selected it. Then, when he looked it up, he saw that Saint Margaret of Scotland was the daughter of Edward the Exile."

"Oh, that's right!" Christine exclaimed. "My mother was an amazement."

"Well, I have to go, Mom," Kora said. "But, I just wanted to say one more thing. The greatest blessing of all of this was when you said recently that each morning you pray that God will somehow use you in the day ahead, and that you have been praying the Novena to the Infant of Prague for many years. I am just so thankful that God gave me a mother who prays. And a father who prays, too. I wish everyone could be fortunate enough to have parents and grandparents who pray. Let's keep spreading the word."

"Yes," Christine agreed. "I always pray for you, Jake, and your children. I have a long list—as my mother did. I hope everyone will learn to pray for their children, grandchildren, and neighbors. For me, having a mother who prayed was God's greatest blessing on earth."

Acknowledgements

We both want to thank Guy, Pete, Cathy, Josh, Jake, Amy, Judge, Kale, Sarah, and all of our loving family and friends for supporting us during this book adventure. We have each of your individual names in our minds and hearts. Thank you for checking in on its progress and for cheering us on!

Thank you also to those who helped with editing, formatting, and publishing: William Moulton, Kale Hiller, and Linda Martin. You were all a big encouragement to us.

From Kate— To my mom, as my five-year-old self said, "You are the prettiest and most fun mom on earth." My older self adds, Thank you for your constant prayers and for showing what it means to live a life of joy and purpose.

From Chris— With heartfelt gratitude for her creative genius, thoughtfulness, and time, I thank my precious daughter, Kate. In the past two years, we have been on an adventure of a lifetime. Full of discoveries, laughter, and the best part of all, lots of quality time together.

And a loving tribute to my dear son, Jake, a true blessing during this journey, who was always there for us.

In loving memory of John Paul, Timothy Edward, and R. Paul Baker. No words can express our heartache ~

HUNTING AND FISHING
WHERE, WHEN AND HOW
BY Joe Dearing
Tues., Dec. 14, 1954   25